W9-CTS-341

THIS BOOK CONTAINS:

THE BORED-TO-DEATH STAR
A SNAIL TRANSLATOR
DETECTIVE TEENY
THE SLOP-PERONI PIZZA OVEN
WINDSHIELD WIPERS
THE QUEEN OF ENGLAND
AND
A MYSTERY!

Read the book. Find the clues. Level up.
Can you handle the awesomeness?
Well, what are you waiting for? **TURN THE PAGE!**

FUN FACT!

You can find all the Awesome Dog
adventures in these books!

#1 *Awesome Dog 5000*

#2 *Awesome Dog 5000
vs. Mayor Bossypants*

#3 *Awesome Dog 5000
vs. the Kitty-Cat Cyber Squad*

AWESOME DOG 5000

5000

vs. MAYOR BOSSYPANTS

JUSTIN DEAN

A Yearling Book

Copyright © 2020 by Justin Dean

All rights reserved. Published in the United States by Yearling, an imprint of Random House Children's Books, a division of Penguin Random House LLC, New York. Originally published in hardcover in the United States by Random House Children's Books, a division of Penguin Random House LLC, New York, in 2020.

Yearling and the jumping horse design are registered trademarks of Penguin Random House LLC.

Visit us on the Web! rhcbooks.com

Educators and librarians, for a variety of teaching tools, visit us at RHTeachersLibrarians.com

The Library of Congress has cataloged the hardcover edition of this work as follows:
Names: Dean, Justin, author.
Title: Awesome Dog 5000 vs. Mayor Bossypants / Justin Dean.
Other titles: Awesome Dog 5000 versus Mayor Bossypants |
Awesome Dog five thousand vs. Mayor Bossypants
Description: First edition. | New York: Random House, [2020] |
Summary: "When Awesome Dog's heroics gain media attention,
Marty, Skyler, and Ralph find themselves targeted by the
narcissistic mayor of Townville" —Provided by publisher.
Identifiers: LCCN 2019019284 | ISBN 978-0-525-64485-9 (hardcover) |
ISBN 978-0-525-64487-3 (lib. bdg.) | ISBN 978-0-525-64486-6 (ebook)
Subjects: | CYAC: Robots—Fiction. | Dogs—Fiction. | Adventure and adventurers—
Fiction. | Mayors—Fiction. | Science fiction.
Classification: LCC PZ7.1.D3985 Awm 2020 | DDC [Fic]—dc23

ISBN 978-0-525-64488-0 (pbk.)

Printed in the United States of America
10 9 8 7 6 5 4 3 2 1
First Yearling Edition 2021

This one's for Stephanie.

The best part of my story.

CHAPTER 1

IT IS THE YEAR 3002, and the galaxy is at war for the second time. . . .

The alien slime ninjas are really mad about losing the last war and have launched another attack on Earth. To ensure victory, they've created a new superweapon: an enormous laser. It's the size of an asteroid, with enough firepower to turn Earth into . . . a really boring planet! This ultimate weapon is known as the Bored-to-Death Star.

In one zap, Earth will instantly become extremely dull. Thrilling hockey matches will make people yawn, yummy ice cream sundaes will taste like chalk, and all pants will transform into khaki slacks. There's only one man who can stop it. . . .

SHERIFF TURBO-KARATE!

The sheriff is back with his special attack: infinity farts! He's ready for the most rootin'-tootin' video game adventure yet! When there's trouble in the galaxy, this hero rises to the challenge!

And it's got a chuck wagon full of bonus extras, including a new set of playable characters! Choose from Deputy Slap-Cheeks, General Frowny Face, Astro-Lobster, or even the president of Earth. She lays down the law with a roundhouse kick of democracy!

SHERIFF TURBO-KARATE 2: THE EMPIRE SLIMES BACK

Twice the karate! *Twice* the action!
The *single* best video game ever made!

**COMING SOON TO A VIDEO GAME STORE
NEAR YOU, FOR ONLY $29.99—**

"Ralph! What are you doing?"

Ralph Rogers didn't look over to his friend Skyler Kwon as she rode up on her skateboard. Ralph was on his scooter with binoculars pressed to his eyes. He was scoping out something down the block. At the bus stop, a teenager was watch-

ing the *Sheriff Turbo-Karate 2* game trailer on his phone.

"I got distracted by the new ad for *Sheriff Turbo-Karate 2*. This game is going to be next level. Here, check it out, Skyler!" said Ralph. He offered her his binoculars.

"Not now," she said. "We're supposed to be helping with the search. Did you see which way it went?"

Just then, a little robot with a propeller on its head zipped past. Skyler pulled a walkie-talkie from Ralph's backpack. She pressed the call button. "Marty, we have eyes on the spybot. It's flying east down Oak Street."

"Copy that, Skyler. We are on our way," a voice squawked back on the walkie.

There was a sonic boom in the sky. Awesome Dog 5000 jetted by, with Marty holding his leash. The chase was on—

Okay. Wait a second. We might need to do one of those book warning thingies.

BOOK WARNING!

If you're reading this book and have no clue what's happening, who these three kids are, or what *Sheriff Turbo-Karate* is, there's a perfectly good explanation for this. This is actually the *second* book about Awesome Dog 5000. Our apologies if there was any confusion. For those who need it, we have prepared a helpful refresher on all the stuff that happened in the first book. If you have read the first book, please skip ahead to the section on spybots located on page 12. Don't worry, you won't be missing much.*

---

* Disclaimer: You will miss the following: the backstory, the occasional joke, foreshadowing, trivia about snakes, a picture of a rabbit with a giant butt, and pages 8–11.

GUIDE TO AWESOME DOG 5000'S FIRST BOOK

So you've decided not to skip ahead to the next section! You must be interested in learning more about Awesome Dog 5000, or maybe you enjoy looking at rabbit butts. Either way, fantastic!

The following is a brief recap to get you all caught up on Awesome Dog 5000. This will take only a few minutes of your time, so sit back and get comfy. May I offer you a tasty beverage before we begin? Water, lemonade, chocolate milk?

Just kidding. I'm a book! Get your own drink. Here we go!

This is Marty Fontana. He's ten years old and new in town. Marty is a huge fan of the video game *Sheriff Turbo-Karate*, and so are his best friends, Ralph Rogers and Skyler Kwon. Together, the three kids make up the Zeroes Club.

Skyler is a punk-rock daredevil who likes to skateboard. Ralph is supersmart and shouts out random trivia like this: "Fun fact! King cobras are the only snakes that keep their eggs in a nest!"

The Zeroes Club discovered Awesome Dog 5000 in Marty's new house. The kids had no idea how he got there, but they quickly learned all about the dog's cool gadgets, like his mega-cannon and rocket paws. Awesome Dog is a lot of fun, but also kind of reckless. Like the time he accidentally crashed into a mansion. It was owned by the evil mad scientist Dr. Crazybrains. This set off a huge battle in his laboratory, where the doctor turned himself into a giant bunny with a twenty-foot-tall rear end—

Yes. You read that correctly.

His butt was humongous.

EVOLUTION OF BUTT SIZE

Awesome Dog defeated the doctor-bunny by blasting him into outer space. When the kids returned home, Awesome Dog led them to an underground room in his doghouse. Its wall of screens showed that someone had been watching their adventure. Thirty different spybots had been secretly recording them the whole time!

Ever since then, Marty, Skyler, and Ralph have been tracking down the spybots. The kids are

hoping to learn who sent the robots, but so far they've never been able to capture one intact. Here's a quick rundown about the thirty spybots:

THIRTY-SPYBOT RUNDOWN

Spybots #2, 5, 8, 9, 10, 12, 18, 19, and 27 were run over by traffic while being chased. The spybots always forget to look both ways when crossing the street. Spybot #3 fell into a lake and couldn't swim. Spybots #4, 6, and 11 blew away on a windy day. Spybot #7 was very lucky. It won the lottery, retired from spybotting, and was never seen again. Spybot #13 was very unlucky. It tripped over a black cat, broke a mirror, and was struck by lightning. Spybots #14 and 15 crashed into each other. Turns out Spybot #16 is allergic to peanut butter (don't ask how). Spybot #17 caught fire while sunbathing by the pool. Spybots #20 through 26 were crushed when Dr. Crazybrains's mansion exploded. Spybot #28 ran out of battery power. Spybot #29 was attacked by a crazed raccoon, and Awesome Dog blew up spybot #30.

This only left spybot #1. It was the kids' last chance to find out who had been recording them.

And that brings us back to the start of this book, where Marty, Skyler, and Ralph are chasing spybot #1 through the neighborhood.

CHAPTER 2

SPYBOT #1 ZOOMED ACROSS the city with Awesome Dog and Marty hot on its tail. Awesome Dog was fast, but the spybot was incredibly agile.

The spybot took a quick right around a big blue mailbox on the sidewalk. Awesome Dog followed but cut the turn too close. He clipped the mailbox's side. It exploded in a flurry of envelopes. Marty was trying his best to steer Awesome Dog,

but yanking on a leash isn't an accurate control system.

The spybot zigzagged between houses and across backyards. Then it hooked a sharp left down a dead-end street. When Awesome Dog rounded the corner, the spybot was nowhere to be seen.

"Hold up, Fives," said Marty. "Fives" was the new nickname the Zeroes Club had decided on for their pet. It was way better than the first nickname they had tried, "A-Doggie-Dog Five Grand."

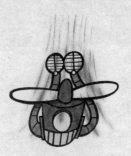

Fives powered down his thrusters and landed on the sidewalk. Just then, Ralph caught up on his scooter. He was sweating and out of breath. Keeping up with a rocket-powered dog is exhausting.

"Did you lose him?" huffed Ralph.

Marty shook his head. "That little sneak is hiding here somewhere."

The spybots were designed to camouflage themselves. They could contort their bodies to blend into any environment. There were a ton of places to hide on the dead-end street: trash cans, shrubs, garden gnomes—and one very suspicious fire hydrant.

Marty pressed his finger to his lips. He gave

Awesome Dog a "shh," then pointed at the fire hydrant. Marty whispered, "Grab that spybot, Fives."

"BARK. BARK. CAPTURING SPYBOT," said Awesome Dog.

His rocket paws ignited. He shot forward in a blur. Suddenly, the hydrant revealed its true form. The spybot's propeller popped out of the top of its head. Its arms snaked out from its sides. Awesome Dog flew in and bit onto the spybot's wrist to hold it in place. The spybot's propellers spun faster as it tried to escape. Awesome Dog clenched his jaws. The spybot slowly lifted itself—with Awesome Dog attached—off the ground.

Marty grabbed on to Awesome Dog's leash. He leaned back to try to pull the pair down, but the spybot was still gaining altitude. Then Ralph dove onto Marty's ankles. That kept the spybot from going higher, but not from moving forward. The spybot towed its three unwanted passengers across a front yard. Ralph was dragged face-first through a bed of flowers. He yelled in between spitting out petals, dirt, and leaves: "I—*pfft*—can't—*pfft*—hold—*pfft*—on—*pfft*—much—*pfft*—longer!"

CRACK! The spybot was swatted down with a heavy smack of a skateboard. Skyler had shown up just in time. The spybot wobbled through the air, puffing out smoke. It chirped a few wonky beeps and bloops before it dropped to the lawn.

"Sorry I'm late," said Skyler. "I passed that kid watching the *Sheriff Turbo-Karate 2* trailer on his phone. You're right, Ralph. That game is really going to be next level."

The Zeroes Club had caught their first spybot. It was finally time to get some answers.

CHAPTER 3

Time for Some Answers
(and a Kung Fu Fight)

THE KIDS GATHERED around the downed spybot. Its eye screen was dark.

"Okay. So what do we do with it now?" Skyler asked her friends.

Ralph picked up the spybot. He gave a mean scowl and yelled, "SPILL THE GOODS, OR WE'RE GOING TO BRING THE PAIN!"

"Whoa! Take it easy, Ralph!" said Marty.

Ralph dropped the act. He smiled and said, "Oh. I was just messing around. I saw a tough guy say that in an action movie once. I thought it sounded cool."

The spybot made a beeping

sound, and a smiley-face icon popped up on its screen. Its speaker trumpeted *toot-too-too*.

A voice announced, "CONGRATULATIONS! YOU HAVE SUCCESSFULLY LOCATED ALL THIRTY SPY-BOTS! A CERTIFICATE OF COMPLETION WILL BE SENT TO YOU IN THE MAIL! GOODBYE!"

The spybot's screen clicked to black again.

"A certificate?!" exclaimed Skyler. "We chased down thirty of these junk buckets, and all we get is a piece of paper?!"

Ralph noticed something on the side of the spybot. It was a connection port. "Ya know, if we hook it up to a computer, I might be able to access the spybot's memory and figure out who made it," he said.

"You know how to do that?" asked Marty.

"Not yet, but after I read and memorize some

library books about computers, I should be able to do it," explained Ralph.

"Wait. You memorize the books you read?" asked Marty in amazement.

Ralph shrugged. "Of course. Doesn't everybody?"

Just then, an old woman wearing thick black-rimmed glasses shuffled out onto her porch. She gripped her walker for support. The granny cried out, "My marigolds! What on earth did you do to my precious marigolds?!"

When the kids had caught the spybot, they had also accidentally uprooted the granny's prized flowers. She had spent months expertly crafting her garden. Three kids and a robot dog had wrecked it in seconds.

The old woman squinted at Marty, Ralph, and Skyler. She shrieked, "Oh dear! Garden goblins and their crazed dog are attacking the neighborhood!"

The granny flew into a rage. She tore her walker apart. Then she used her pearl necklace to tie the two metal bars together. She swung the makeshift nunchucks around her body.

Granny Nunchucks shouted, "I WAS A KUNG FU MASTER BACK IN THE DAY! YOU GOBLIN TROUBLE-MAKERS ARE ABOUT TO GET DEALT WITH!"

"Wait! We can explain," said Ralph.

"There's no time to apologize, Ralph. We have to get out of here right now," said Marty.

Marty knew they were responsible for the mess in the garden, but it was easier to run away than to face the consequences. The kids grabbed Awesome Dog's leash and spybot #1. They rocketed away before Granny Nunchucks actually did bring the pain.

CHAPTER 4

In Control

MARTY, SKYLER, AND RALPH had converted the secret room under Awesome Dog's doghouse into the Zeroes Club's official headquarters. They called it HQ-0. They decorated it with Sheriff Turbo-Karate posters, added a minifridge stocked with juice boxes, and put in a shelf for Ralph's collection of rocks that look like Abe Lincoln. They even rewired the wall of thirty screens so they could watch movies on it.

Ralph had been spending time in HQ-0 after school. He was trying to hack into spybot #1's memory drive. When Marty and Skyler stopped by to check on his progress, Ralph was unscrewing the spybot's circuit board. Behind him were stacks of library books with a range of titles from *Robotics for Dum-Dums* all the way to *Programming for Brainiacs*.

Marty looked over the collection and asked, "You read *all* these this week?"

"Yep," said Ralph. He tapped the screwdriver to his forehead. "And they're all in the noodle."

Ralph had what's known as a photographic memory. He could read up on any topic and instantly become an expert. After only a couple of days, Ralph was now a computer whiz.

"Ralph's brainpower is turbocharged," Skyler said to Marty. "If you ever want to see a cool trick, ask him to name every critter from Chi-Chi-Mookipon."

"That's ridiculous. No one can do that from memory. The Chi-Chi-Mookipon cards have like a thousand different critters," said Marty.

"Fun fact! Chi-Chi-Mookipon has five thousand eight hundred ninety-one unique critters," said Ralph.

"Well, five thousand eight hundred ninety-two if you count the rare platinum card for Skitch Skootle."

Marty's jaw dropped. From now on, he was definitely going to ask Ralph to help him study for tests.

Ralph connected a cable from the spybot to the television wall's console. He typed on a computer keyboard. The screens filled with scrolling numbers.

Ralph explained. "So I logged into spybot's mainframe, but all the stored data is encrypted behind a firewall."

Marty and Skyler looked at each other in confusion.

Ralph simplified it. "The spybot's computer is locked. There's no way to figure out who sent the robot," he said.

"Locked?!" Marty yelled in frustration. "This spybot was our last hope to solve the mystery, and now we have nothing to show for it!"

"Well, not nothing. There is some good news," said Ralph.

He tapped return on the keyboard. The thirty screens changed to a single image. It showed the backs of the kids at that very moment.

"You found another spybot? Where is it?" asked Skyler.

She spun around to see Awesome Dog staring back at her. Ralph patted Fives on the head and said, "I figured out how to copy spybot number one's programming! Then I downloaded it into Awesome Dog."

"BARK. BARK. SAY CHEESE!" said Awesome Dog.

"You gave him camera eyes?! That's so cool!" said Marty. He busted out a goofy pose with a peace sign and stuck his tongue out.

"The camera is only one component," said Ralph. He turned to Awesome Dog. "Fives, let's go for a walk."

"Go for a walk" was the command to make Awesome Dog fly. His retractable leash unspooled from his collar. Ralph picked it up and plugged it into his handheld video game system, the Funstation. The game screen showed real-time video from Awesome Dog's perspective. It had a headsup display with speed, battery power, and radar. It was like playing an Awesome Dog flight simulator.

"I know Awesome Dog's difficult to steer, so I made him a controller," said Ralph.

He pushed the start button, and Awesome Dog's rocket paws ignited. Ralph pressed the up option on the directional pad. Awesome Dog hovered off the floor.

Skyler begged for the controller. "GIMME! GIMME! GIMME! I'VE GOT TO TRY THIS OUT!"

Ralph handed it over. He explained, "I made it easy to use, too. I've mapped all the buttons. The A button accelerates, and the B button slows down."

"What's C do?" asked Skyler, but she didn't wait for an answer. She immediately hit the button.

"`BARK. BARK. MEGA-CANNON ACTIVATED,`" said Awesome Dog. His eye lights switched to crosshairs. The hatch in his back opened. A huge bazooka popped out.

"Can we please *not* blow up anything today?" asked Marty. He tugged at Fives's leash to pull him down, then jammed the mega-cannon back into its chamber. "Awesome Dog has been getting us in too much trouble lately. We just smashed up the neighborhood and ruined that granny's garden. Sooner or later, somebody is going to start looking for us. To be safe, I think we need to lie low and keep Fives a secret."

And from that moment on, the kids never, ever let anyone in the world find out about Awesome Dog.

C'mon. Who are we kidding? Obviously, everyone found out about Awesome Dog. The title of this book isn't

THE THREE KIDS
WITH A SECRET THING
NO ONE KNOWS ABOUT

CHAPTER 5

Mayor Bossypants

ACROSS TOWN AT CITY HALL, the mayor was having a new suit made for himself. An assistant was tailoring the suit to the mayor's body while two other assistants held up a giant mirror. For nearly three hours they had been trying to give the mayor the perfect style he demanded, and he demanded a lot.

The mayor of Townville was named Manny Bossypants. He had a white fluffy doodle of hair and was about as tall as the average fourth grader. He tried to hide his smallness by going big with everything. He drove a monster truck, ate jumbo shrimp for lunch, and always wore oversized suits with superwide shoulder pads.

The mayor even had a large number of assistants. His team of pint-sized helpers did every task he ordered. The mayor never bothered to learn any of their names, though. Instead, he referred to them as the teeny-tinies. They were a group of men and women even shorter than the mayor, dressed in identical suits and wearing different hats that matched their specific jobs. For example, the Construction Teenies wore hard hats, the Cook Teeny wore a chef's hat, and the Plumber Teeny wore a

red cap with an "M" across the front. He also had a mustache and loved mushrooms for some reason.

Secretary Teeny entered the office. He was carrying a folder and had a nervous look on his face. He said, "Sorry to interrupt, sir, but I just received this report from the police. An old woman claims three goblins and their dog attacked her house and flew away."

"Ugh, I don't have time to deal with goblins," groaned Mayor Bossypants. "I have like a zajillion million other way more important things to do for the city today."

This was a lie—and not just because he made up the number zajillion million. Mayor Bossypants never did anything important for the city. The only thing Mayor Bossypants cared about was himself. And today's work schedule.

9:00 A.M.   Wake up. Slap the snooze button.

9:08 A.M.   Wake up. Eat a big breakfast.

10:00 A.M.   Have the teeny-tinies make me a
new suit.

1:00 P.M.   Lunch at the seafood restaurant
Titanic Diner.

2:00 P.M.   Attend my statue extravaganza.

3:00 P.M.   Stare at my ant farm and feel
gigantic.

5:00 P.M.   Watch the cartoon show
Chi-Chi-Mookipon.

"Yes, sir. We all know you are very busy, but the police believe this goblin attack might be part of a bigger problem," said Secretary Teeny.

He showed the mayor the police file. A photograph of Dr. Crazybrains was paper-clipped to the first page. Secretary Teeny continued. "A few weeks ago, this scientist's mansion blew up. The neighbors said they saw a dog fly out of it before it exploded. These two incidents—the old woman and the mansion—may somehow be connected, Mr. Mayor."

Mayor Bossypants swiped the report. He thumbed through the pages before asking, "And what happened to the mansion's owner? This Dr. Crazybrains?"

"The police aren't sure," said Secretary Teeny. "The doctor could be on Jupiter for all they know. I think it best we postpone your statue's reveal today until we—"

"NO! NO! NO! I WANT MY STATUE EXTRAVA-GANZA!" Mayor Bossypants pouted. He threw the file down and stomped on it. "I WANT IT! I WANT IT! I WANT IT! AND I'LL HOLD MY BREATH UNTIL I GET IT!"

The mayor took a big gulp of air and clamped his mouth shut. He always threw a tantrum when he didn't get his way.

Nurse Teeny rushed in. She pleaded, "Mr. Mayor, please, you have to breathe!"

The mayor closed his eyes, crossed his arms, and wagged his head no. His cheeks puffed out. His skin turned pink from the lack of oxygen. His body started to twitch. He was about to pass out.

Secretary Teeny said, "Okay, okay, we'll do the event today, exactly as you wanted, sir."

The mayor let out a huge exhale, then took a breath. The color returned to his face.

"Good," said Mayor Bossypants. "I'm glad you realized that I was right and you were acting childish. Now, Candy Teeny, bring me a lollipop! I deserve a treat for being such a good boy!"

CHAPTER 6

Large and in Charge

MANNY BOSSYPANTS had won the election for Townville mayor because he promised voters he would do three things:

Create new jobs! Clean up the city! And help the needy!

It was a landslide victory for Manny Bossypants. Everyone voted for him because those are three great ways to improve the city, and he kept all three of his promises. It just wasn't how any of the citizens expected.

On his first day in office, Mayor Bossypants ordered the construction of a new city project. He named it the Legendary Look-at-Me-No-Seriously-Look-at-Me Statue Extravaganza. The monument would be in honor of none other than Mayor Bossypants himself.

It was a hundred-foot-tall shiny steel version of the mayor. It was equipped with dozens of features, including a laser light show, stereo speakers, firework launchers, and a T-shirt cannon that hurled souvenir shirts with the mayor's picture on the front. The statue even had a hologram projector. It played 3-D images of people cheering. A ring of high-powered fountain jets encircled the monument.

Mayor Bossypants hired a brigade of teeny-tinies to build his statue and all the extras that came with it. That was how the mayor fulfilled his first promise. He *had* created new jobs . . . but all the jobs were for the teeny-tinies.

The next thing the mayor did was have his workers bulldoze First Street. Every shop was leveled and paved over. That was how the mayor

fulfilled his second promise. He *had* cleaned up the city . . . by making it a parking lot for his statue.

Mayor Bossypants did all of this for one selfish reason. He desperately wanted people to think he was a big shot. Having a town celebration for his giant statue would make everyone have to look up to the little man and admire his greatness. He had helped the needy—which in this case was himself. The mayor needed everyone to know that he was epic.

Unfortunately for the mayor, on the day of his statue's reveal, something even more epic caught the town's attention.

CHAPTER 7

Ready Player None

THE ZEROES CLUB was in a funk—and not the cool kind of funk that makes you good at dancing. This was the gloomy kind of funk that makes you frown at rainbows. The kids had been obsessed with solving the spybot mystery, and with the last one gone, they never got any real answers. For weeks, it had been the only thing they were focused on—well, maybe not the *only* thing.

Today was the release of *Sheriff Turbo-Karate 2*. If there was anything that would get the kids in the good, dancing kind of funk, it was kicking slime ninjas into star dust. They'd had a blast beating the first game and were pumped to play the sequel.

Marty, Skyler, and Ralph had pooled together thirty dollars from their piggy banks. They went downtown to the video game store and picked up a copy of *Sheriff Turbo-Karate 2* from a display in the shape of a cowboy hat. The box art showed all the new in-game content.

"Holy moon cheese!" said Ralph. "You can drive vehicles now?! There's a pony hoverbike!"

"They've got new skins for the sheriff, too! I am definitely getting these cute butterfly wings and the demon-skull mask," said Skyler.

"Sorry, but that stuff's only on the gold deluxe edition," a store employee said. He was a lanky teenager wearing a Funstation T-shirt and a name tag that read KEV.

Kev showed the kids that *Sheriff Turbo-Karate 2* actually had two versions of the same game. The MEH EDITION was $29.99, which they could afford, but the GOLD DELUXE EDITION was $99.99— way out of their price range.

"The game trailer never said anything about a gold deluxe edition," said Ralph.

Marty grabbed a copy of the meh version. The small box was made of cheap cardboard and didn't have any game images on it. There was just the title, spelled wrong, hand-written in crayon.

"We don't *really* need all the extras," said Marty. "I'm sure the regular version is just as fun."

"Trust me. It's called the meh edition for a reason," warned Kev. He counted on his fingers all the reasons it was terrible. "It only has single-player mode, it only has the tropical island level, you can't use jump kicks, and the sheriff's default costume is a garbage bag. It's like the game is literally calling you trash for not getting the gold deluxe edition."

Skyler tossed the game box onto a shelf and said, "What a rip-off! We barely scraped together thirty bucks! How are we supposed to get another seventy?"

The kids decided to save their money until

they could buy the gold deluxe edition. They left the store empty-handed. It was another defeat for the Zeroes Club.

"We had the whole day planned out to play *Sheriff Turbo-Karate* 2. What are we supposed to do now?" asked Marty.

Skyler gave a nod across the street. "That could be fun."

Mayor Bossypants's statue extravaganza was about to start.

CHAPTER 8

The Legendary Look-at-Me-No-Seriously-Look-at-Me Statue Extravaganza

MARTY, SKYLER, AND Ralph joined the crowd at the statue's reveal. The monument was draped in a colossal sheet and wrapped in a red ribbon with a bow on the front.

"Fun fact! Leonardo da Vinci designed a helicopter in 1480," said Ralph.

He looked up at the helicopter flying overhead. It was from the popular magazine *Epic Human Monthly*. Each issue featured people who had done the world's most epic things. This month there would be a cover story on the mayor. The helicopter was here for aerial photos of the event.

Mayor Bossypants ran onto the stage in front

of the statue. He gave a little wave up to the helicopter. Then he addressed the crowd. "Citizens of Townville—and, more importantly, *Epic Human Monthly,* whose staff I personally invited—it is my honor to present the greatest achievement any city has ever seen: the Legendary Look-at-Me-No-Seriously-Look-at-Me Statue Extravaganza! You will be amazed at how epic I am—I mean, it is!"

Mayor Bossypants ordered Oversized-Scissors Teeny to cut the statue's ribbon.

The sheet dropped, revealing the monument. An electric-guitar chord played. The fountain jets spritzed some water. Then a T-shirt cannon fired a souvenir into the crowd. Red and blue lasers blinked once, and a single firework fizzled in the air. A group of the statue's prerecorded holograms clapped and said, "Hooray."

And that was it.

The crowd scowled up at the statue in silence. No one was impressed. The people of Townville thought the extravaganza was really an extrava-waste of time, space, and money.

"I thought it would be bigger," some guy in the crowd muttered.

Mayor Bossypants was furious. He dashed over to the statue's control panel and swatted away Stage-Manager Teeny. The mayor cranked the celebration dial to ultra-mode.

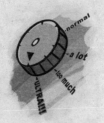

Rock music blasted so loud that it blew people's hair back. The fountain jets erupted into geysers before raining down on spectators. Hundreds of fireworks exploded in the sky like it was a war zone. The T-shirt cannon switched to rapid fire. It pelted the crowd with wadded-up shirts. The cheering holograms grew into scary screaming giants.

The crowd panicked. They took off running, but the wet pavement caused them to slip, slide, and crash into each other. The parking lot was full of human bumper cars.

Safety Teeny, wearing an orange vest, hurried up onto the stage. He shouted over the chaos: "PLEASE, MR. MAYOR! YOU HAVE TO STOP THIS! SOMEONE'S GOING TO GET HURT!"

"I DON'T CARE ABOUT PEOPLE GETTING HURT!" the mayor yelled back. "THE WORLD HAS TO KNOW I'M EPIC!"

Suddenly, the helicopter above was struck by a firework and burst into flames. The pilot jumped out just before the helicopter exploded. He landed on top of the statue's hair and rolled down the forehead. He quickly grabbed on to the statue's bottom lip. He held tight as his feet dangled.

"Help me!" yelled the pilot. "My hands get really sweaty when I'm in dangerous situations or when I have to speak in public! Both of which I'm doing right now! Please hurry! I'm going to slip off!"

If someone didn't act quickly, the pilot would fall a hundred feet. Skyler turned to Marty and said, "We have to get Awesome Dog."

CHAPTER 9

Awesome Dog Comes to the Rescue

"NO WAY," SAID MARTY. "Do you see how many people are here, Skyler?" Marty wanted to help the pilot, but using Awesome Dog would expose their secret. "I'm sure someone else will save him."

"That is highly unlikely," said Ralph.

A group of firefighter teenies huddled under

the statue, reading an instruction booklet. They were frantically trying to assemble a large trampoline to catch the pilot. Unfortunately, they'd forgotten to bring the right type of wrench.

"There isn't time to wait for someone else," said Skyler. "We have to do something *now*."

Marty craned his neck up at the statue and said, "Maybe if we—"

But Skyler was already rolling away on her skateboard. She called back over her shoulder, "If you won't get Awesome Dog, I will!"

Skyler raced through the neighborhood, taking every shortcut she knew. She skated into Marty's backyard, ditched her board, and took the doghouse elevator down to HQ-0.

ALL-MART

START

"Let's go for a walk, Fives," she said. "We're going to play catch."

"BARK. BARK. STARTING WALK PROGRAM."

Skyler plugged the Funstation controller into Awesome Dog's leash and hit start.

Back at the statue, a flock of pigeons had landed on the pilot's sweaty hands. Their tails were in his face. When he turned away, a feather tickled his nose.

"ACHOO!" The pilot sneezed. His wet palms slipped off the smooth steel. He dropped from the statue. The pilot screamed in terror as he fell toward the pavement. He covered his eyes as he—

Soared back up into the air!

The pilot peeked through his fingers to see that he was flying. Fives had swooped in and caught him by his jumpsuit collar just in time.

"That's how it's done, Fives!" said Skyler.

But she had spoken too soon.

SSHHH-POW! A high-powered fountain jet smacked Awesome Dog under his chin like an uppercut. He was tossed sideways and dropped the pilot! Luckily, they were close to a rooftop, and the pilot landed safely.

Fives began flying erratically. He swerved up and down. He jerked left and right. Skyler tried to steady him, but none of the controller's buttons responded. Water had seeped into Awesome Dog's circuits. He had a super-advanced computer system, but it wasn't completely waterproof. The Funstation screen flashed an airplane icon.

"BARK. BARK. FLIGHT CONTROL ERROR. BARK. BARK. ENGINE FAILURE," said Awesome Dog.

The light in his eyes flickered. His turbo boosters sputtered, then cut out completely. Awesome Dog tipped into a nosedive.

Skyler screamed out, "AAAAAAAAHHHH!"

Then she saw they were going to crash into a fluffy pillow warehouse below. It was going to be a soft landing.

Skyler let out a sigh of relief.

Then she saw a sign that read GRAND OPENING NEXT YEAR! The pillow warehouse was empty. It was going to be tough landing after all!

Skyler screamed again. "AAAAAAAAHHHH!"

Awesome Dog crashed through the warehouse ceiling. He bounced and skidded across the concrete floor. Luckily, Skyler was wearing her skateboarding pads. She only suffered some scrapes and bruises.

When they came to a stop, Skyler pulled off her helmet and asked, "You good, Fives?"

Awesome Dog shook and twisted his body like a real dog whipping water off his back. Two windshield wipers swished across his eyes. After drying out his circuits, he said, "BARK. BARK. PLAYING CATCH IS FUN."

CHAPTER 10

Marty Has a Meltdown

WITH ALL THE MAYHEM at the statue extravaganza the day before, Marty was ready for a nice, calm morning at school. He could focus on his book report, play basketball, and not worry about Awesome Dog.

But when Marty took his seat in Mrs. Taylor's class, he overheard two students talking behind him.

Annie Markowitz said, "My friend's mom's dentist was in the front row when it flew by. He thinks the army's testing a top-secret project. It was a dog-shaped jet, and the person holding the leash was the pilot."

Bobby Figgins disagreed. "Nu-uh. An expert on the news said it's an undiscovered species of bird. They're calling it the beagle eagle. The person behind it wasn't a pilot—it was a bird-walker."

The mysterious flying dog had become the talk of Townville, but Marty wanted no part of the conversation. He quickly pulled out his math book and studied a random page, pretending to read the lesson. He was trying to avoid any questions about Awesome Do—

"Hey, Marty, what do *you* think that flying thing was?" asked Annie.

Marty went pale. His heart raced. He panicked and blurted out the first thing that came into his head: "ACUTE ANGLE!"

The first thing that came into Marty's head was the math lesson in front him. It was on triangles. Annie and Bobby were puzzled. Marty tried to cover by saying, "I meant a . . . cute . . . angel. Yeah. Like a little baby-cheeked angel flying around with his wings. Looking cute."

Bobby shook his head and said, "You're such a dork, new kid."

A few weeks ago, being called a dork would have bothered Marty. But he didn't mind it so much anymore. Now he saw it as a badge of honor. Being labeled the "d" word meant he was in good company with the other school dorks, his two best friends, Skyler and Ralph.

For lunch, Marty got a tray of gross cafeteria "food." "Chunk-shaped with a scoop of gray" was

on today's menu. He joined Skyler at table #0. Marty asked her, "Did you know that the entire school is talking about Awesome Dog?"

"I know! Isn't it cool?" said Skyler with the flash of a smile. "It's like we're superheroes!"

Marty whipped a glance over both his shoulders to make sure no one was listening. He turned back with a shout-whisper: "Hey! Keep it down!"

"Don't stress. No one has a clue it was us. Fives and I were going so fast that all the photos and videos anyone got were too blurry to see my face. Besides, do you really think someone can catch Awesome Dog?" asked Skyler.

Marty didn't share her confidence. He was on edge. His hands nervously shook as he fumbled to open his chocolate milk carton. Just as he took a sip, Ralph popped out behind him and yelled, "HOLY MOON CHEESE!"

Marty choked on his drink and snorted milk out his nose. All he could smell was chocolate.

"Hey! What's the big deal, Ralph?!" asked Marty.

Ralph pulled a paper out from his hoodie pocket and said, "When I was returning some books to the library, I saw this flyer posted on the bulletin board."

He slapped the paper down on the table. Across the top, it read:

NIKOLA TESLA ELEMENTARY SCHOOL
1ST ANNUAL SCIENCE FAIR!

Ralph tapped his finger on the page. "*This* is the big deal!"

Marty and Skyler looked down at the flyer.

Marty asked, "The big deal is it's . . . 'SPONSORED BY ALL-MART'? What's so great about that, Ralph?"

"Sorry." Ralph slid his finger to a different spot. "I meant *this* is what the big deal is!"

The science fair's grand prize was in bold print: **BEST INVENTION WINS $100.**

"HOLY MOON CHEESE! A HUNDRED BUCKS!" exclaimed Marty. "If we win this contest, we can buy *Sheriff Turbo-Karate 2: Gold Deluxe Edition!*"

CHAPTER 11

Going for the Gold

THE KIDS SPENT LUNCH brainstorming inventions for the science fair. The most obvious idea was to enter Awesome Dog, but that would definitely reveal their secret.

Ralph laid out the strategy. "All we have to do to win the grand prize is come up with the absolute best invention ever thought of in the history of science and technology."

"Sounds easy enough," joked Marty.

"No. We can do this," said Skyler. "Remember, guys, there's no such thing as a bad idea."

This is what the kids came up with:

A crossbow that fires
snapping turtles

A top hat with a cuckoo clock
in it

A computer mouse shaped
like a cat

Disposable paper socks

Popcorn-flavored soda

Or soda-flavored popcorn—
either way you'll only need
one treat at the movies

A pocket-sized toaster
for waffles on the go

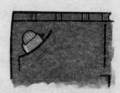

A sleeping bag with sewn-in
legs so you can walk around
in it

A compass that points
to the nearest compass

"I was wrong. These ideas are terrible," said
Skyler. She slouched in her seat, defeated. There
wasn't a worthy invention in the bunch.

The school bell rang. Lunch was over, and it was time for recess. Shades, the leader of the cool kids, passed by table #0 on his way out. He noticed that the Zeroes Club's trays were still full of "food." They had been so busy brainstorming, they forgot to eat.

"Not hungry for slop today, dork patrol?" asked Shades.

The rest of the cool kids laughed, following Shades out of the cafeteria. Cool kids at Nikola Tesla Elementary always brought sack lunches. Only dorks like the Zeroes Club ate cafeteria food.

That's when a big, bright lightbulb clicked on inside Marty's brain. He swiped his fork and began shaping his "food." First, he molded some gray goop into a triangle. Then he flattened two green chunks into small circles and placed them on top of the triangle. It looked like a slice of pizza!

Marty asked, "What if we invented something that made cafeteria food cool?"

CHAPTER 12

Epic Fail

FOR THE FIRST TIME EVER, *Epic Human Monthly* didn't feature a human as the cover story. This month's headline was FLYING ROBOT DOG SAVES THE DAY! It had a photo of a fuzzy white dot rescuing the magazine's helicopter pilot. On the bottom right corner of the cover, another story was listed: ALSO A STATUE THING HAPPENED . . . BUT WHATEVER, WHO CARES.

Awesome Dog had upstaged the mayor, and Mayor Bossypants was very upset about it. Actually, "very upset" was putting it nicely. The mayor threw his biggest tantrum yet. He went "cray-cray ba-donkers sandwich." (And yes, that is the official medical term. Though not as severe as "cray-cray ba-donkers sandwich with extra mustard, no lettuce.")

The mayor ordered the teeny-tinies to buy every copy of *Epic Human Monthly* in the city. Next, he had them rip the magazines into little pieces and craft a papier-mâché minivan. Then Mayor Bossypants drove over it with his monster truck.

But none of that made the mayor feel any better. He was still angry.

He called a meeting to scold his workers. "Why didn't one of you warn me about this flying dog?!

If I had known about it, I would have waited to do my statue extravaganza!"

The teeny-tinies *had* warned Mayor Bossy-pants about Awesome Dog back in chapter 5. Unfortunately, Librarian Teeny didn't have the book you're reading now as proof.

Nurse Teeny said, "On the bright side, that pilot is going to be okay."

"SO WHAT?!" screeched the mayor. "The only thing that matters to me is ME! No one will know how epic I am as long as this stupid pooch is in town—wait, I've got it!"

With a snap of his fingers, the mayor ordered, "OFFICIAL MEMO!"

A teeny-tiny handed him a piece of paper. Another teeny-tiny gave him a pen. A third dropped to his hands and knees, creating an instant desk with his back. The mayor pulled up a chair and started writing.

"I'm declaring a new law!" Mayor Bossypants said. "From now on, all dogs are to be arrested, dressed in ugly sweaters, and exiled to the top of Mount Everest!"

Desk Teeny looked over his shoulder and offered an alternative. "Sir, rather than sending all the dogs to a mountain in Asia, perhaps you could capture this *one* dog."

Mayor Bossypants considered the idea for a moment. Then he exclaimed, "Yes! I'll capture this *one* dog! What a smart idea I just came up with!"

The mayor pulled an extra copy of *Epic Human Monthly* from his coat pocket and tossed it to an assistant. He said, "You, Detective Teeny, find me this dog so I can destroy him!"

"Jolly good!" said Detective Teeny. He had an English accent and wore a hat like Sherlock Holmes's. Detective Teeny examined the magazine cover. He slowly traced his finger across the photo, drawing a line from Awesome Dog to a building below. "Hmm. Based on my knowledge of aerodynamics, I would deduce it crashed in this fluffy pillow warehouse. I shall begin the investigation forthwith!"

Mayor Bossypants snapped his fingers at another assistant. This one was wearing a backward baseball cap and a sleeveless suit that showed off his massive biceps. The mayor issued his order: "Toughstuff

Teeny, go with Detective Teeny in case there's trouble, but keep the job *hush-hush*. I can't risk that dog getting any more press."

The two teenies headed to the fluffy pillow warehouse to search the crash site. It didn't take long for Detective Teeny to find the first clue. Directly below the hole in the ceiling were dusty footprints on the floor. Detective Teeny used his magnifying glass for a closer look.

"Aha! These treads are from skateboarder shoes," he said, stroking his chin. He then selected a ruler from his detective bag to measure the shoeprint. "Interesting. The length is of child proportion. Perhaps a fourth—no, fifth—grader."

He sniffed the footprints and nodded. The feet weren't stinky. Detective Teeny knew they couldn't be a boy's shoes.

"THINK FOUND DOG!" announced Toughstuff Teeny. He was holding a brick.

Toughstuff Teeny was a bit dim. His muscles were so big that they drained all the blood from his brain.

"No, that's not a dog—that's a piece of the smashed ceiling. However, if I'm not mistaken, you've revealed another clue," said Detective Teeny.

He drew a pair of tweezers from his kit and plucked a single strand of hair off the brick. The hair was purple.

"It appears to solve this case," Detective Teeny said with a smirk. "We need to locate a fifth-grade girl who skateboards and has purple hair. It's elementary . . . school, my dear teeny!"

"THINK FOUND DOG!" announced Toughstuff Teeny again. He had picked up another brick.

CHAPTER 13

Test Run #796

THE IDEA for the Zeroes Club's invention was as simple as it was brilliant. Disgusting cafeteria food would go in one side of a machine and come out the other side as delicious pizza.

1.   **2.**   **3.**

To build it, the kids collected spare parts from their parents' old hair dryers, alarm clocks, toasters, and radios. Skyler had the best creative eye, so she designed the invention's exterior. She gave it a sleek case with cool lightning bolts along the sides. Ralph created the inner machinery by reading up on flamethrowers, chemistry, and Italian food recipes. Marty was tasked with naming the invention. After he presented a list of options, the kids agreed on the Slop-peroni Pizza Oven.

There was just one final step: making the invention actually work. The kids had kept a video journal of all their failed attempts. It was the best way to learn from their mistakes, and there had been plenty of them—795 to be exact.

"BARK. BARK. I AM RECORDING . . . AND AC-TION!" said Awesome Dog. His camera eyes were focused on Ralph.

"Okay. This is test run number seven hundred and ninety-six," said Ralph. "After test seven hundred and ninety-five's failure, I've made a slight adjustment to the cooking burners. Fingers crossed the flames stay inside the machine this time."

When Ralph turned around to begin, he unknowingly showed off black grill marks across the seat of his pants. He told Marty, "Insert the food sample, please."

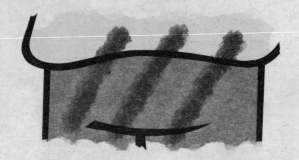

Marty tipped in a plastic container of his mom's leftovers. The green meat loaf wasn't as bad as cafeteria "food," but after a month in the fridge, it was close enough. Marty gave Skyler a nod.

She pulled a lever. The oven rumbled and hissed. Steam shot out of the sides. A piercing white light glowed through the cracks. There was a loud roar. Then . . .

A little bell dinged. The food was ready.

Ralph scowled at the output slot. He said, "Fun fact: Thomas Edison failed a thousand times before he created the lightbulb."

"Aw, man," said Marty. "I was really hoping it worked this time."

Ralph pulled a slice of pizza from the machine. The green meat loaf had been transformed into a cheesy slice of pizza. Ralph cheered, "Good thing we're not making lightbulbs! We've got our first official slice! Woop-woop!"

The kids had done it! Test run #796 was a success!

"I call first bite!" said Skyler. She grabbed the slice and bit into it. She immediately grimaced and spit it into a trash can. "Uwk! It's even worse than regular cafeteria food. It tastes like a mixture of burnt tuna fish and black licorice."

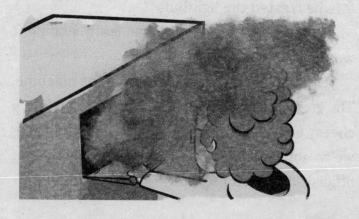

Ralph opened the oven's side hatch to check the problem. A plume of smoke billowed out. The burner jets were completely melted. There was no way to convert slop into pizza without them.

"We've used up all our spare parts. How are we going to replace four flame jets?" asked Marty.

"BARK. BARK. SHOULD I BE RECORDING THIS?" asked Awesome Dog.

Skyler gave a big grin. The solution was right in front of them. She said, "Guys, we need four jets. Awesome Dog has four rocket paws!"

Ralph pondered the idea. "I mean, it wouldn't be that difficult. I could create an adapter for his collar and plug him into—"

"No, no, no," interrupted Marty. "We are not taking Awesome Dog to school!"

Skyler nodded and sarcastically said, "You're right, Marty. It is *way* too risky. We should quit the science fair and just buy the meh edition of *Sheriff Turbo-Karate 2*. We can still have tons of fun taking turns in single-player mode . . . as a hero in a trash bag!"

Marty thought about how awful it would be to save the galaxy dressed as garbage. He agreed to use Awesome Dog, but on one condition. "We have to make sure, no matter what, to keep Fives completely out of sight the entire time," he said.

The kids did an amazing job hiding Awesome Dog inside their invention. No one at the science fair had any idea he was powering the Slop-peroni Pizza Oven.

That is, until the two teeny-tinies showed up.

CHAPTER 14

A Teeny-Tiny Little Problem

THE SLOP-PERONI PIZZA OVEN was a great idea, but winning the school science fair wasn't going to be easy. When Marty, Skyler, and Ralph got to the school gym, there were already rows and rows of amazing science fair inventions.

Rashid Patel's team had made Wherever Skates, which squirted ice from the toes so you could ice-skate anywhere. Carlos Cruz had created the Attracto Glove: with a simple snap, small metal objects could be pulled into the palm. You'd never have to search for your car keys again! The most bizarre invention, though, belonged to a group of kids known as the Snail Squad. They'd invented the Shell-epathic Helmet. It was a brain scanner that translated snail thoughts into spoken English.

Skyler wasn't intimidated by the competition. "C'mon, boys," she said, skateboarding over to their table. "Let's get cooking!"

The Zeroes Club got to work setting up their booth. Skyler decorated it with informative posters on the history of lunch, Ralph installed the Slop-peroni Pizza Oven, and Marty wheeled in a barrel of cafeteria "food" he had borrowed from the lunch ladies.

When the fair's judges came to inspect their invention, Ralph gave a quick peek inside the oven hatch. He whispered, "You ready, Fives?"

Awesome Dog's rocket paws heated up. He said, "BARK. BARK. POWERING COOKING JETS."

Skyler announced to the judges, "We present to you the Slop-peroni Pizza Oven! It's the coolest new way to eat cafeteria food!"

She pointed to Marty. He took her cue and scooped a serving of "food" into the oven.

Skyler continued her explanation. "Gross stuff goes in there. Then the machine mixes up the food's atoms, changing its flavor and shape. Next, it's perfectly heated at exactly four hundred seventy-five degrees until it transforms into . . ."

Skyler trailed off. She was distracted. Across the gym, there was a nine-foot-tall man in a trench coat. He was wearing a fedora on top of a Sherlock Holmes hat and had a very fake beard. He awkwardly swayed to keep his balance as he walked. The strange man had the head of Detective Teeny and the arms of Toughstuff Teeny. Beneath the coat, his legs were actually stilts with shoes on the bottom. The mayor had told the teenies to be discreet, and this disguise was . . . well, it was something.

The teeny tower was on a direct course for Skyler.

Nothing was going to get in the teenies' way, not even the cool kids. When Shades walked in front of them, Toughstuff Teeny pushed him aside.

"OUTTA WAY, SUNGLASS FACE!" he said from inside the coat.

Detective Teeny's eyes were laser-focused on Skyler. He was like a shark slowly coming in for a bite. Skyler couldn't take her eyes off the towering weirdo. He was stalking closer . . .

and closer . . .

and closer . . . until—

Ding! The little bell sounded from the Slop-peroni Pizza Oven. It snapped Skyler's attention back to her presentation. She said, "We're done for—I mean, it's done. Disgusting slop becomes delicious pizza."

Marty and Ralph served up some slices from the machine. The judges each took a bite and wrote down their scores. Skyler gave them a polite smile. As soon as the judges walked away, her smile dropped. She turned to her friends and said, "Guys! There's a weirdo at the science fair, and I think he's coming for us!"

"What makes you think that?" asked Ralph.

A long shadow fell over Skyler.

"Well, if it isn't a purply-haired skateboarding fifth grader. You've crossed the wrong man, and now you've got some explaining to do," said Detective Teeny.

Toughstuff Teeny cracked his knuckles and flexed his giant biceps.

From one of the nearby booths, a snail wearing a little helmet said, "OH SNAP! THOSE KIDS ARE IN TROUUUUUUUUUUBLE!"

CHAPTER 15

Double Trouble

MARTY, RALPH, AND SKYLER tilted their necks all the way back to look up at Detective Teeny. It was like they were sitting in the front row of a movie theater that was showing a scary movie about a tall weirdo who had buff arms and was wearing two hats.

"You are in possession of something I want," said Detective Teeny.

Marty was pretty sure the weirdo wanted Awesome Dog. Instead, Marty offered a slice of pizza. "Is the thing you want a cool new way to eat cafeteria food?"

Toughstuff Teeny grabbed the slice and repeatedly punched it to a cheesy pulp.

"Fun f-f-f-fact," Ralph stuttered. "Pizza was invented by . . . a person . . . in a year . . . I don't know." Ralph was so terrified, his photographic memory had completely blanked.

Detective Teeny got to the point. "I've been sent to put an end to your superhero dog. So where is this metallic mutt of yours?"

Skyler wasn't going to give up her friend so easily. She said, "Even *if* we had a superhero dog, we'd protect him forever! You could search for a million years and never find where we've hidden him!"

"BARK. BARK. THE MACHINE IS OVERHEATING. POWERING DOWN MY ROCKET PAWS," Awesome Dog said from inside the Slop-peroni Pizza Oven.

Detective Teeny chuckled to himself. Completing the mayor's assignment was going to be as easy as pie—or in this case, pizza pie. Toughstuff Teeny ripped the invention open.

Awesome Dog looked up with his tongue wagging. He greeted the teeny-tinies: "BARK. BARK. HELLO. I AM AWESOME DOG 5000."

From under the trench coat, Toughstuff Teeny drew out a pole with a net at the end. He tossed the dogcatcher net over Awesome Dog.

"Okay, Awesome Dog. Now we're going to walk out of here nice and easy," said Detective Teeny.

Marty did a facepalm. He muttered under his breath, "I really wish you hadn't said 'walk.'"

"BARK. BARK. STARTING WALK PROGRAM," said Awesome Dog.

His paws switched to rocket boosters and blasted off, pulling the dogcatcher net with him. Detective Teeny and Toughstuff Teeny held on to the pole and were jerked forward at breakneck speed. The trench coat blew open, and the stilt legs were left behind.

Awesome Dog shot into the middle of the science fair, dragging the teenies behind him. They tore through a row of booths before smashing through a wall and into the bathroom next door.

The teenies lost their grip on the net and were flung across the room. They crashed into a toilet stall. Awesome Dog landed and started wagging his tail. He had no idea they were bad guys. He was just having fun.

But Toughstuff Teeny was going to put an end to that. He quickly rolled off Detective Teeny. He bowed out his chest and balled up his fists, ready to fight. He threatened Fives: "ME CLOBBER DOG!"

"BARK. BARK. SELF-DEFENSE MODE ACTI-VATED," said Awesome Dog. His missile launcher opened and targeted Toughstuff Teeny.

Toughstuff Teeny dropped his hands. "Uh . . .

ME SORRY, DOG. ME HIDE NOW." He slowly walked backward into the toilet stall and shut the door.

Marty, Skyler, and Ralph ran into the school bathroom. Awesome Dog was still holding his aim. When they opened the stall door, it was empty. The toilet had been ripped out of the floor by Toughstuff Teeny. The two teeny-tinies had escaped down the broken pipe and into the sewers.

CHAPTER 16

The Unusual Suspects

THE ZEROES CLUB managed to sneak out of the bathroom—through the door, not the sewer . . . that's gross—before anyone at school saw them. They returned to HQ-0 to wrap their heads around what had just happened. They also needed some refreshments. Being threatened by evil henchmen was stressful! Juice pouches were required.

"There's definitely something fishy going on," said Skyler.

"Oh, I think you're just smelling Awesome Dog. He was splashed by some toilet water," said Marty.

"No, not that," said Skyler. "That weirdo said he was 'sent to put an end to' our superhero dog. I don't want to get ahead of ourselves, but if those two were ordered to take out a superhero, that can mean only one thing: they're working for a supervillain."

Marty gave her a blank stare. Skyler couldn't be serious. So he told her, "Skyler, you can't be serious."

"It's not such a wild theory, Marty," said Ralph.

"If our encounter with Dr. Crazybrains taught us anything, it's that supervillains hate Awesome Dog. I've put together a list of some possible suspects who might have a grudge against him."

Ralph wheeled out a bulletin board. It was pinned with photos, note cards, and little plastic bags of evidence. Lines of red string tied them all together.

"Whoa! That's the real deal!" said Skyler.

"Yeah. I just so happened to have read a book on the FBI earlier this morning," said Ralph.

He flicked off the room's light switch. Awesome Dog's eyes automatically turned on like two spotlights. Ralph pointed to a picture on the board and said, "Suspect number one: Granny Nunchucks! We destroyed her flower bed. She has a motive for revenge, plus skills in weapon crafting, two supervillain qualities. She's old, bold, and stone-cold evil!"

"No, she's not," argued Marty. "She's a grandma whose garden was ruined by three reckless kids. *We're* the bad guys in that scenario."

"Mmm. Good point," said Ralph. He x-ed out the picture with a black marker. He continued to the next photo. It was their classmate Shades. Ralph explained, "Suspect number two! We all know Shades hates us. Somehow he must have discovered we're the owners of Awesome Dog, and he is taking his vengeance."

"That doesn't make any sense," said Skyler. "The weirdo guys pushed Shades out of their way at the science fair. They wouldn't have done that if he was their boss."

Ralph frowned. He put an X through Shades's picture, too. Then he sidestepped to the last photo and circled it with the marker. "That leaves only our PRIME SUSPECT!" he declared. "The queen of England! Dun-dun-dun!"

He flicked Awesome Dog's eye lights on and off over the queen's picture. It was a very dramatic effect.

Skyler arched an eyebrow and asked, "Why would the supervillain be the queen of England?"

"It's the perfect plot twist!" said Ralph. "No one would ever expect the evil mastermind to be the queen of England"

"Okay, I've heard enough," said Marty. He turned the room lights back on. "These guys are probably looking for Awesome Dog because he smashed something of theirs. This is exactly why we need to stop bringing Fives out in public."

"No, we just need to be more responsible when we do, Marty," said Skyler. "Now that Fives has a controller, he should be out there in the world saving the day, not stuck down here getting dusty."

Marty wanted some backup. He asked, "Ralph, you agree with me, right?"

Ralph glanced to Skyler, then back to Marty. He delicately said, "Well, I . . . kinda agree with Skyler. I mean, if you remember, the box we found Awesome Dog in was labeled 'A.W.S.M.' It stood for the Autowork and Service Machine. I think the whole reason Fives was built was to help people."

Marty threw his hands in the air in disbelief. "Do you two have any idea what can happen if we pick a fight with a supervillain? Do you remember what Dr. Crazybrains was like? We barely survived a mansion exploding that time," he said.

Skyler pointed to the poster on the wall and said, "C'mon! Sheriff Turbo-Karate didn't hide when the alien slime ninjas attacked Earth. He flew straight into their moon base and battled their king. No matter how scary or difficult the challenge, heroes don't run away. They rise to the challenge."

"Well, this isn't a video game," said Marty. "And we're not heroes."

"Speak for yourself, Marty." Skyler pushed past him toward Awesome Dog. "Let's go for a walk, Fives," she said.

"BARK. BARK. STARTING WALK PROGRAM."

Awesome Dog's leash rolled out. Skyler reached for it, but Marty quickly swiped it away from her.

"He's not going anywhere, Skyler. We're in enough trouble as it is," said Marty.

"Last time I checked, you weren't the boss of Awesome Dog." Skyler reached out for the leash again, but Marty pulled it away.

"He's *my* dog. I found him at *my* house. I'm in charge of him."

"You're being really selfish, Marty," said Skyler.

"And you're being a real idiot, Skyler," he snapped back. "Awesome Dog stays here in the doghouse. If you don't like my rules, you can go home."

Skyler stepped back in shock. There was hurt in her eyes. She couldn't believe how her best friend was talking to her. She opened her mouth, but no words came out.

Ralph shot a stern look at Marty and said what Skyler didn't: "Not cool, dude. Not cool."

"You heard him, Ralph. Let's go home," said Skyler.

Skyler and Ralph turned and went to the elevator. Marty instantly regretted what he'd said. He didn't really want his friends to leave. He was just frustrated and scared. Marty ran toward them and called out, "Wait. I didn't mean tha—"

But it was too late. The doors closed. His friends were gone. Marty stood alone in the silence.

After a moment, Awesome Dog walked up behind him. Fives asked, "BARK. BARK. ARE WE STILL GOING FOR A WALK?"

Marty shook his head. With a heavy heart, he said, "Sorry, boy. No more walks."

CHAPTER 17

Out of the Blue

MAYOR BOSSYPANTS had blocked off his entire schedule to dice up new copies of *Epic Human Monthly* with his lawn mower. Decorator Teeny placed magazines on the office carpet. The mayor furiously pushed the mower around, kicking up a blizzard of shredded white paper.

It was only September, but DJ Teeny played holiday music on his turntables. The mayor lay on the floor and made snow angels in the paper scraps while his assistants built a magazine snowman. Hot-Cocoa Teeny wheeled his cart in and handed out warm drinks. Santa Teeny and his Elf Teenies set up a workshop to make toys. The winter wonderland came to an abrupt end when Detective Teeny and Toughstuff Teeny burst into the office. Their clothes were sopping wet. They looked terrible and smelled worse.

After escaping through the bathroom pipe, they had swum through a mile-long river of sewage to get back to city hall. They were dripping dirty water.

Mayor Bossypants didn't care what had happened to them. He had only one question: "Sooooo where's the dog?"

Detective Teeny wrung the sewage out of his hat as he said, "We were bested by the canine."

The mayor pouted. "No! No! No! That's not fair!"

He went into a frenzy, swinging his lawn mower around his office. He sliced up his collection of self-portraits. He chopped up his bookshelf of personal autobiographies. Then he hacked up the file cabinet of blueprints for the hundred-foot-tall statue of himself.

"How could you two let this happen? You're the smartest and strongest assistants I have!" yelled the mayor.

Toughstuff Teeny said, "DOG METAL HARD. DOG WIN."

"Huh?" asked the mayor.

"Perhaps I should clarify," said Detective Teeny. "This robot is called Awesome Dog 5000, and for good reason. He's as fast as a jet and as strong as a battleship. He's got a tank cannon. Apprehending him will require a super-soldier."

The mayor asked Secretary Teeny, "Do I have a Super-Soldier Teeny on the payroll?"

The assistant checked his clipboard, then shook his head.

"Ugh! I never get what I want!" groaned the mayor. He began pacing around his teenies. "If I'm going destroy this Awesome Dog, I'll need some serious firepower. Something so big, something so strong, something he'll never see coming. Something—" The mayor stopped.

He had caught a look at himself in the giant

mirror his two Fashion Teenies were holding. A shredded strip of a blueprint was hanging over part of the glass.

"Something . . . like me," Mayor Bossypants said.

In a moment of complete, random coincidence, the statue's fountain jet design was covering the right half of the mayor's reflection. It appeared as if Mayor Bossypants had a mechanical arm.

His lips curled into a deranged smile. Mayor Bossypants was going to have the teeny-tinies make him a new suit.

CHAPTER 18

Awesome Mayor 5000

THE TOWNVILLE POLICE had received a report of vandalism on First Street. When three cop cars arrived on the scene, they found the Legendary Look-at-Me-No-Seriously-Look-at-Me statue in ruins. All the steel plating had been stripped off and the gadgetry torn out. It had been reduced to a broken metal frame with sparking wires. A demolition crew of teeny-tinies were packing up their jackhammers, saws, and drills. They had just finished the job.

One of the cops called out, "Everybody, freeze! You are all under arrest for destruction of public property!"

A loud voice boomed from the sky, "I prefer to think of it as recycling!"

SHOOOSH! A massive figure rocketed in with fireworks spraying from the soles of its metallic boots. It landed with the force of an earthquake and shattered the pavement. It was Mayor Bossypants. He was in a giant mechanical robot suit that also kind of looked like a regular business suit. It was terrifying yet stylish.

"Pretty neat, right?" asked the mayor. He did a twirl to show off his new outfit while he explained his upgrades: "The teeny-tinies converted my statue's equipment into high-tech battle armor. I've got laser-targeting eyesight, a hydro-jet arm blaster, a shoulder-mounted T-shirt cannon, a hologram projector, firework rocket boots, and a whole list of other goodies. You know what? It's probably easier if I just show you."

His arm blaster doused an officer with a fire-hose stream of water. The cop was flipped back into the air and landed down the block. The police were not equipped to handle giant-robot attacks. They dove behind their cars for cover.

The robo-mayor power-jumped into the air, then dropped onto a squad car. With an explosive *KA-CRUNCH!* the vehicle flattened to a pancake.

"OH! YEAH! BEING A GIANT MANIAC ROBOT IS SOOOO MUCH FUN!" cheered Mayor Bossypants.

The cops took off on foot. The robo-mayor's laser guidance locked onto them. His shoulder cannon fired a cluster of extra-extra-extra-small T-shirt balls. The tiny souvenir shirts were like homing missiles.

The shirts closed in on their targets, then popped open and slunk over the cops' heads and down onto their bodies. The officers' arms were squished flat to their sides. Every officer fell to the ground, squirming in the incredibly tight-fitting fabric. They could barely breathe, let alone move.

"Good gravy!" exclaimed Granny Nunchucks. She had been walking to the All-Mart when she saw the police officers being attacked. She clutched her chest and said, "First garden goblins and now evil cyborgs! This city is getting way too dangerous for a woman my age!"

Mayor Bossypants chuckled. That granny had given him the perfect idea of how to catch Awesome Dog. He called for Secretary Teeny and asked, "Do we still have that police file on the garden goblin attack?"

CHAPTER 19

A Blast from the Past

THE OCEAN TIDE WASHED Marty onto the beach. He coughed up some seawater before rolling over onto his back. He squinted up at the pizza-shaped clouds floating by. Then he looked at the cowboy boots on his feet.

Marty found himself on a deserted island. It was all very confusing. Marty had no idea where

he was, how he had gotten there, or what was up with his footwear.

When Marty stood up, he noticed Awesome Dog's leash on the sand. It was extended out and led back into the island's inner jungle. Marty followed the leash to the entrance of a cave that was shaped like a doghouse.

Marty cupped his hands around his mouth and yelled, "Fives! You in there?"

A pair of evil red eyes popped open in the darkness. They were definitely not Awesome Dog's. Marty turned to escape, but three slimy green tentacles whipped around his boots. The tentacles coiled tight and pulled him back by his legs. He couldn't run away now.

A beast emerged from the shadows. It was a . . .

GIANT!

BLOB MONSTER!

WITH THE FACE OF . . .

THE QUEEN OF ENGLAND!

Marty gasped awake. He wasn't on the island anymore. He was in his own bed at home. Marty peeked under his covers. Socks. No cowboy boots. He let out a huge sigh of relief. It had only been a nightmare.

Marty shook the weird thoughts out of his head and checked his alarm clock. It was 8:00 a.m. on Saturday. He went downstairs, poured himself a bowl of Atomic Choco-Bites, plopped down on the living room couch, and watched TV as he ate.

Chi-Chi-Mookipon was on. A boy in a blue baseball cap, Chase O'Card, was hugging two critters.

One of the creatures was a koala thing wearing glasses. The other was a parrot thing with a plume of purple feathers.

Chase beamed a big happy smile and said, "I'm so lucky to have two of the bestest of best friends like you, Fuzzlebub and Chirpaloo! There's nothing more valuable in this world than friendship!"

A knot formed in Marty's stomach. He quickly changed the channel. It was a news broadcast.

"This just in," the reporter said. "Three Townville police officers have gone missing this morning. Their best friends are very concerned for them because that's what best friends do. They care for one another—"

Marty groaned and changed the channel again. A commercial for *Sheriff Turbo-Karate 2* was on. The announcer said, "And wrangle up your posse for co-op mode because playing with friends is way better than being alone!"

A team of three sheriffs rocketed through space. They were on a collision course with an army of attacking slime monsters. The sheriffs called out in unison, "When there's trouble in the galaxy, heroes rise to the challenge!"

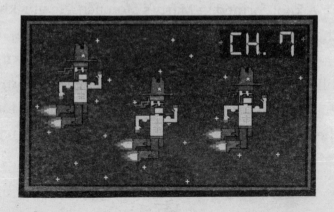

Everything was reminding Marty about his fight with Skyler. He couldn't take it anymore! He clicked the TV off. That's when he heard barking outside. Marty went to check it out.

Awesome Dog was in the front yard, barking nonstop. His ears were laid back.

Marty asked, "Fives, what's wrong? What're you doing out of the doghouse?"

"BARK. BARK. MAJOR THREAT DETECTED," said Awesome Dog.

Marty followed Awesome Dog's line of sight. What waited across the street wasn't just a major threat. It was a nightmare, but Marty wasn't dreaming this time.

Dr. Crazybrains had returned.

Wait. Hold up. This part could use a book warning.

BOOK WARNING!

Did you just scream in your mind, "Dr. Crazy-brains?! Are you kidding me?! You can't have a new villain pop up in chapter 19! This story already has Mayor Bossypants and all those teeny-tinies. And don't forget about the granny! It's crowded enough without adding yet another bad guy! This is like trying to stuff a winter coat into your sock drawer."

If so, you, my smart reader, are correct.

While it does seem like the main villain from the first book has just randomly appeared more than halfway through the story, don't worry. This will make total sense—well, as much sense as you can expect in a book with a robot dog, a nunchuck-swinging granny, and a video game sheriff with fart powers.

Okay. So, at best it will make medium sense.

Also, you might want to chill out a little when reading a book. Screaming so much in your mind is bad for your health. It will give you a headache.

CHAPTER 20

The Return of Dr. Crazybrains

MARTY COULDN'T BELIEVE his eyes. Dr. Crazybrains was back! The mad scientist wagged his finger in the air and yelled, "I'LL GET MY REVENGE ON YOU!"

"BARK. BARK. MARTY PROTECTION MODE ACTIVATED," said Awesome Dog. He ran at full speed toward the doctor.

Dr. Crazybrains pointed and said, "I'LL GET MY REVENGE ON YOU! I'LL GET MY REVENGE ON YOU! I'LL GET MY REVENGE ON YOU!"

The doctor kept repeating himself. Every time he spoke, he did the same finger wag. It was like he was stuck in a time loop. Marty quickly realized something wasn't right. He chased after Awesome Dog and called out, "Whoa, whoa, whoa! Wait a sec, Fives!"

The warning came too late. Awesome Dog was blindsided by an extra-extra-extra-small T-shirt. The shirt slid over his head and onto his torso. The fit was so tight that it squeezed Awesome Dog's front legs against his body. Awesome Dog face-planted into the sidewalk. He tried to get up, but he was wrapped tight.

The robo-mayor jumped out from his hiding spot in the tree. A light beam projected from his robotic suit's chest. Just like the 3-D images of the fans at the mayor's statue, Dr. Crazybrains was just

a hologram. The mayor had learned all about Dr. Crazybrains from the police report. He knew the doctor would be the perfect bait to catch Awesome Dog off guard.

The robo-mayor slapped a button on his chest. The doctor dissolved into pixels. Mayor Bossypants bragged, "Now, that is what you call an EPIC trap!"

Marty stumbled back and fell to the ground in fear. He recognized the mayor from the statue extravaganza, but seeing him as a souped-up cyborg was frightening.

The mayor picked up Awesome Dog, looked him square in the eyes, and said, "I'm going to enjoy getting rid of you, *Awful* Dog 5000. First, I'm going to crush you. Then I'm going to twist you. Then I'm going to sculpt you into a neat little hood ornament and mount you on the front of my monster truck. HA! HA! To the junkyard!"

The mayor rocketed away with Awesome Dog. Marty sprinted back to his house and upstairs to his bedroom. He grabbed the walkie-talkie off his desk and radioed his friends.

"Mayday! Mayday! SOS! 911! This is a red-alert emergency! Zeroes Club, do you copy?! Awesome Dog has been captured! Repeat. Awesome Dog has been captured! We have to get to the city junkyard to save him! There's not much time."

Marty released the call button. He waited for a response.

No one answered.

He pleaded again. "Does anyone copy? Ralph? Skyler? Anyone? We have to rescue Fives! Please . . . I can't do this by myself."

But all Marty heard was static.

CHAPTER 21

It All Goes to Junk

WITHOUT HIS FRIENDS, Marty had to embark on a lone rescue mission. He rode his bike to the edge of town and pedaled up to the junkyard entrance. It was a creepy archway made of twisted metal. Beyond it, ghastly towers of crushed cars stabbed into the sky. Somewhere in all that wreckage, Mayor Bossypants was holding Awesome Dog prisoner.

Marty took a deep breath. He was ready for this. It was no different from the final moon level of *Sheriff Turbo-Karate*—

Except this was real.

And terrifying.

And he was about to fight a maniac robo-mayor.

Okay. This was nothing like the moon level. Marty wasn't ready for this at all.

He left his bike at the gate and made his way into the junkyard maze. Each turn led to another corridor of scrap metal. Soon all the gray blended together. Marty kept moving forward until he noticed a bright cherry-red convertible among a stack of cars. It was the third time he had seen it.

Great. Marty was lost! He had been walking in circles. He had no idea where Awesome Dog was, or even if there was still time to rescue him. Marty hung his head, and his shoulders slumped.

"Another great job," he said to himself. "Way to mess up yet again."

From around the corner, he heard a slow, menacing . . .

SHHHHHH!

SHHHHHH!

SHHHHH!

Something big was shuffling toward Marty. It came closer and closer. Its shadow grew larger and larger. Marty backed away in fear. It had to be Mayor Bossyp—

Nope. Never mind. It was just Ralph wearing a shrub costume.

"RALPH?!" said Marty in complete and utter surprise. "What are you doing here?"

"You called for help," said Ralph. "It woke me up. I tried to answer you, but I couldn't find my glasses in time to see where my walkie was. I got here as fast as I could. Fun fact! The Zeroes Club sticks together, no matter what!"

Marty ran over and gave his friend a big hug. The costume's branches poked him in the chest. Marty asked, "Ralph, why are you dressed like a bush?"

"It's his silly rescue-mission disguise," said Skyler, rolling up on her skateboard. "I didn't think he should wear it, but I don't tell my friends what they can or can't do."

She gave Marty a knowing smirk. She wasn't just referring to the costume.

"I'm so sorry, Skyler," said Marty. He went into full apology mode. "You were right about everything: Awesome Dog, the supervillain thing, me being selfish. I was the one being idiotic. I never should have said that stuff to you. I—"

Skyler held up her hand to stop him. "I forgive you, Marty. What you said really hurt, but I know you weren't trying to be mean. We're still friends."

Marty nodded and said, "Always." He couldn't believe he was so lucky to have friends like Skyler and Ralph!

"And as much as I enjoy hearing you apologize for being a jerk," she added, "we have something way more important to take care of right now. We need to find Awesome Dog."

Marty nodded and said, "He's somewhere in the junkyard, but I have no idea how to locate him."

"Found him!" Ralph was looking at his Fun-station. There was a blinking red dot in the center of the screen. "When I installed the controller, I also put in a GPS tracker," he explained. "Thought it might be useful if we ever lost him."

Marty beamed a huge smile. The Zeroes Club was back!

CHAPTER 22

A Not-So-Awesome Rescue

THE RED BLIP on the Funstation screen led the kids to the junkyard's recycling area. There was a teeny-tiny in a welding mask dragging the T-shirted Awesome Dog. This assistant was Hood-Ornament-Maker Teeny.

Marty pulled his friends behind a utility shed. "There," he whispered. "One of Mayor Bossypants's henchmen has Awesome Dog."

Ralph was disappointed. "The mayor's the supervillain?! Aw man! I was really hoping for the queen of England!"

Hood-Ornament-Maker Teeny brought Awesome Dog to a large metal compactor with an attached crane. He set his prisoner down and started the machine.

The magnetic plate at the top of the crane's

arm hummed to life. The teeny-tiny steered it over a metal trash heap. A rusty old motorcycle flew up and out of the pile. It stuck flat to the magnetic plate. The teeny-tiny guided the bike back to the compactor and dropped it in. With the flick of a switch, the motorcycle was slowly crushed.

Hood-Ornament-Maker Teeny gave a thumbs-up and yelled out, "The compactor works great, sir! We're ready to begin whenever you are!"

Marty scanned the recycling area. Who was the teeny-tiny talking to? Marty spotted the mayor's monster truck parked off to the side, but he didn't see the owner.

"Uh, where's the mayor?"

"Right behind you," answered a voice.

The kids slowly turned around to see the robo-mayor. Skyler was awed by his upgrades. "Wowza," she said. "You really maxed out your armor skill points."

"Oh yeah," said Marty. "I forgot to tell you. Mayor Bossypants is a cyborg now."

The robo-mayor's shoulder canon shot an extra-extra-extra-extra-large T-shirt around all three kids. He scooped them up in the blanket of a shirt and power-jumped over to the compactor. He dumped them out onto the ground.

The robo-mayor said, "You three get front-row seats to my newest city project. I'm calling it the Destruction-of-Your-Robot-Dog-Who-Is-

Annoying-and-I-Hate-Him Extravaganza. The name's a work in progress."

"Why are you doing this, Mr. Mayor?" said Ralph.

"Funny you should ask that," said the mayor. "I've prepared an epic slideshow to answer that very question!"

Marty rolled his eyes. "Ugh. Let me guess. This is the part where you tell us a twisted tale of serious evil about why you became a bad guy?"

The mayor frowned and said, "Backstory? What? No! Backstories are so cliché. I'm more interested in the future. MY FUTURE!"

The light from Mayor Bossypants's holo-projector flickered. The "epic" slideshow presentation began.

CHAPTER 23

An Epic Slideshow

"THROUGHOUT HISTORY, few people have been so amazing that they're considered epic," said Mayor Bossypants.

The robo-mayor's holo-projector clicked through a slide presentation of the world's most famous people: it included scientists, presidents, athletes, explorers, movie stars, and even that one guy who could stuff twenty chicken nuggets in his mouth at once.

"And I'm one of them!" said the mayor.

CLICK! The slide changed:

It was a photo of a big, tanned bodybuilder. He had the face of Mayor Bossypants.

"Did you stick your head onto a picture of a muscleman?" asked Skyler.

"NO!" yelled the robo-mayor. His cheeks blushed in embarrassment. "That's totally me with my shirt off. You can't tell because I wear slimming business suits—it doesn't matter! The point is, I am just as epic as the rest of those people, and the world needs to know it!"

CLICK! New slide:

It was the cover of *Epic Human Monthly* featuring Awesome Dog, with a few edits.

The robo-mayor explained. "That cover story was supposed to be about me and my statue! Now no one is paying attention to me, with your dog flying around my town. That's why I'm getting rid of him!"

CLICK! New slide:

It was a drawing of Awesome Dog as a hood ornament on the mayor's truck.

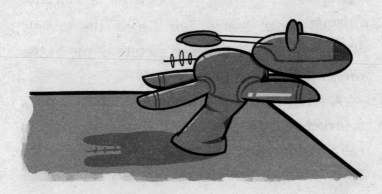

"Then nothing will stop the world from knowing I'm the biggest, the bestest, the most epic-est person in history!" said the robo-mayor.

CLICK! New slide:

The photo showed Mayor Bossypants dressed up as the Chi-Chi-Mookipon critter Skitch Skootle.

The kids giggled. "Real epic, Mr. Mayor," said Skyler.

"Slideshow Teeny!" exclaimed the mayor. "Why is there a Halloween picture of me in the presentation?"

A teeny-tiny with a camera around his neck scurried over. He apologized. "Sorry, sir. You told me to put in a photo of you in the epic suit. Skitch Skootle is the rarest critter. He's very epic, sir."

Mayor Bossypants looked down at his high-tech battle armor, then glared to the slideshow picture of him in a homemade costume.

Slideshow Teeny's eyes went wide. He realized his mistake. "Ooooooh. You meant the epic suit you're wearing *now*! That makes way more sense!"

The mayor told his assistant, "I'm assigning you a new job title. From now on, you're Bird-Watching Teeny."

His assistant was confused. "Uh, you want me to take pictures of birds now?"

The mayor picked up the teeny-tiny in his giant metal hand and said, "Yes. Up close!"

And he threw the teeny-tiny into the sky.

Luckily, the teeny safely splashed down in the local duck pond. He was fine, but his underwear got very soggy.

Mayor Bossypants took a deep breath, cleared his throat, and continued laying out his master plan. "Ahem. As I was saying, with *this* suit, which I am wearing now, my epicness is unstoppable. I don't have to settle for being the mayor of Townville anymore. I can be the mayor of Earth! I'm going to rule the world. I'm going to make everyone my personal assistant! You all will work for ME and do every teeny-tiny job I order!"

CLICK! New slide:

It was a picture of a teeny-tiny with a mug of soda. Marty's face was taped onto the teeny-tiny's. The robo-mayor said, "You'll make my root beer floats!"

CLICK! New slide:

Skyler's face was taped onto a teeny-tiny filling out paperwork.

"You'll do my taxes!" the robo-mayor said.

CLICK! New slide:

A picture of Ralph was taped onto a teeny-tiny painting nail polish onto Mayor Bossypants's toes.

"You'll make my feet look pretty!" said the robo-mayor.

CLICK! New slide:

The projector displayed the robo-mayor overseeing a global army of teeny-tinies.

Mayor Bossypants screamed, "THE WORLD WILL FINALLY KNOW I ... AM ... EPIC!"

His firework boots launched him high into the air as he fist-pumped. The robo-mayor held his pose for a moment before dropping back to the ground. When the dust settled, he noticed that his prisoners were gone.

"Um, where did those kids go?" he asked.

"Right behind you," answered Marty.

Mayor Bossypants turned around to see the kids and the newly freed Awesome Dog. His mega-cannon was pointed straight at the robo-mayor.

"BARK. BARK. TARGET ACQUIRED," said Awesome Dog.

"Mr. Mayor, you can do your own taxes. Get him, Fives!" said Skyler.

Awesome Dog fired his missile. The mayor's lightning-fast robo-reflexes kicked in. He twisted at the waist. The missile sailed past his chest. He immediately grabbed it and threw it right back! Awesome Dog quickly reloaded. He fired another missile to intercept it.

KA-BOOM! The two missiles collided in a massive midair explosion. The shock wave blew the kids off their feet, but the robo-mayor stood tall. His suit was so powerful that he was unfazed by the blast. Mayor Bossypants brushed the ash off his shoulder.

Ralph let out a cough. "Well, that didn't go as planned."

"We don't stand a chance against this guy. Fives, get us out of here," said Marty.

"BARK. BARK. STARTING WALK PROGRAM," said Awesome Dog.

His leash unspooled, and the kids grabbed hold. Awesome Dog fired up his rocket paws—

KERSPLASH!

He was drenched by the robo-mayor's hydro-jet arm blaster. Awesome Dog somersaulted backward, and his paws flamed out. His eye lights blinked as he slowly got to his feet. He shook the water off his body to right himself.

"Sorry! But no one leaves work until the boss gives the word! And the word is 'no'!" yelled the robo-mayor.

Ralph said to his friends, "Those water blasts are messing up Awesome Dog's circuitry. There's no way the mayor's going to let us fly away."

"Okay. Then we try something different," said Marty. He grabbed the Funstation controller out of Ralph's shrub costume's pocket and plugged it into the leash. "Let's rise to the challenge."

Marty pressed start on the controller.

SPECIAL MOVES
➤ MEGA-CANNON
➤ TURBO FLIGHT
➤ WET PUPPY KISSES

SPECIAL MOVES
➤ HYDRO BLASTER
➤ FIREWORKS BOOTS
➤ BABY POUTING

CHAPTER 24

Robo-showdown

SKYLER AND RALPH ducked behind a pile of scrap metal as Marty and Awesome Dog faced off against Mayor Bossypants.

"Wreck this fool!" yelled Skyler.

Marty tapped C on the Funstation, and Awesome Dog repeatedly launched his mega-cannon. Three missiles zoomed toward Mayor Bossypants. In a blur of motion, the cyborg spun, sidestepped, and hurdled over each shot. It was a triple miss.

"I thought you were supposed to be awesome, dog?" said the robo-mayor. Marty mashed the A button, and Awesome Dog's rocket paws launched. He and Marty flew toward the mayor. Mayor Bossypants fired his water blaster, but Marty expertly swerved around the jet stream. Awesome Dog lowered his head and rammed the robo-mayor square in the chest.

Fives drove the robo-mayor across the junkyard. He slammed Mayor Bossypants into the side of his own monster truck. Marty quickly steered Awesome Dog up into a barrel roll. They circled back down and launched a missile before the robo-mayor could dodge.

KA-BOOM! A fiery explosion consumed Mayor Bossypants, leaving a thick haze of black smoke in the air.

Marty landed Awesome Dog next to Ralph and Skyler. The three friends high-fived. Ralph gave a "woop-woop," and Skyler cheered, "You did it, Marty!"

Awesome Dog didn't join in the celebration. His eye lights were scanning the smoke. "BARK. BARK. NEW THREAT DETECTED—CORRECTION. BARK. BARK. NEW *THREATS* DETECTED."

The robo-mayor crawled out from the thick fog. His steel armor was charred. He was wheezing and hacking up dust. He slowly got up to a knee.

Marty held his thumb over the C button. He warned, "It's over, Mayor Bossypants. You lost! You take one step, and you're toast."

"Yeah, but which one of us are you going to blast?" asked Mayor Bossypants.

Another robo-mayor emerged from the smoke. Then another robo-mayor flew in on his firework boots. Another ran in, and another power-jumped over to them. There was another, and another, and another, and another.

Soon there was a legion of identical robo-mayors.

"He can clone himself?" asked Ralph.

"No. He has a hologram projector. Only one of them is real," said Marty.

Marty chose a random robo-mayor and fired. Awesome Dog's missile sailed through the hologram. The image glitched, then disappeared. There was only one way to identify the real mayor: eliminate the impostors.

Skyler shouted, "SPAM THE ATTACK BUTTON!"

Marty tapped C as fast as he could. Awesome Dog unleashed a hail of missiles. Holograms were blown into pixelated bits.

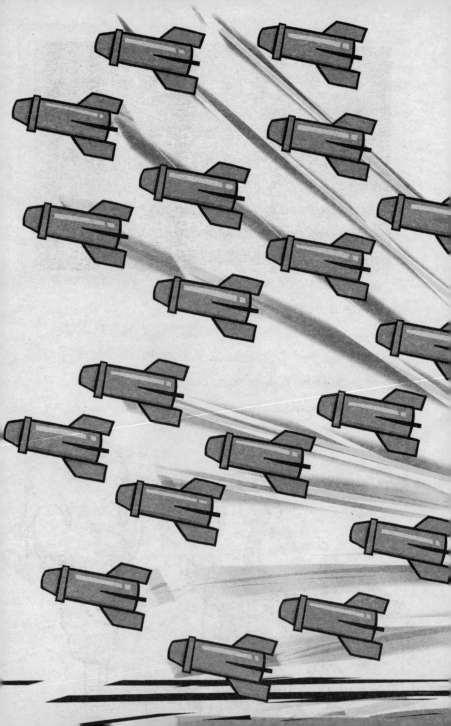

c,c,c,c,c,c,c,c,c,c,
c,c,c,c,c,c,c,c,c,c,
c,c,c,c,c,c,c,c,c,c,
c,c,c,c,c,c,c,c,c,c,
c,c,c,c,c,c,c,c,c,c,
c,c,c,c,c,c,c,c,c,c

KA-BOOM!

KA-BOOM!

KA-BOOM!

KA-BOOM!

Until . . .

KA-CLICK! KA-CLICK! Awesome Dog's mega-cannon was empty. Fives had limited belly storage, after all. A blinking red missile icon flashed on the Funstation's screen.

"BARK. BARK. AMMO DEPLETED," said Awesome Dog.

One of the robo-mayors stepped forward. He deactivated the remaining holograms.

The real Mayor Bossypants grinned. "My turn."

CHAPTER 25

Round Two

THE ROBO-MAYOR was going to put an end to Awesome Dog once and for all.

But first he needed an audience! "Cheering-Section Teenies! Get out here!" he called.

A group of assistants rushed over and set up bleachers. They filled the stands and began clapping and yelling, "Hurray!" Snack Teeny sold hot dogs and popcorn. Cheerleader Teenies cartwheeled in. They pumped up the crowd by chanting, "LET'S GO ULTRA! LET'S GO! LET'S GO ULTRA! LET'S GO!"

The robo-mayor didn't want to disappoint his fans. He cranked the statue dial on his forearm controls to ultra-mode. His robot suit transformed into an even bigger form!

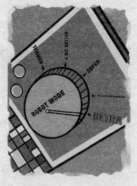

The suit's firework boots doubled in height, making the mayor twice as tall. His body armor replated itself with thicker, bulkier steel. His water blaster converted into a four-barrel bazooka. He was now the ultra-robo-mayor. The teeny-tinies went wild with applause.

The mayor stared down at Awesome Dog and the kids. "Time to teach you all some new dog tricks. First trick: roll over!"

He lifted his arm's quad-zooka and let loose a hurricane. Marty pressed the A button to dodge it, but he wasn't fast enough. A tidal wave crashed over them. The water washed away, leaving Marty with a disconnected Funstation. Awesome Dog was on the other side of the junkyard. He was soaking wet and stumbling around, chasing his own tail.

"BARK. BARK. L-L-LOCKING ONTO NEW TARGET!" stuttered Awesome Dog. "B-B-BARK. BARK. WHY D-D-DOES THE NEW TARGET LOOK LIKE MY OWN BUTT?"

"That's not good," said Ralph. "The water must have shorted out his abductive-logic matrix."

"Yeah, definit— Wait. What's that mean in normal talk, Ralph?" asked Marty.

"Not so scientifically speaking"—Ralph adjusted his glasses—"his brain is scrambled eggs. None of his systems will work properly now. He won't be able to fight back."

"We have to help him," said Skyler.

The ultra-robo-mayor power-jumped over to the defenseless dog. He grabbed Fives by his ears and lifted him up. Awesome Dog's body hung limp as the mayor showed him off to the Cheering-Section Teenies. The fans showered the mayor with applause. They shouted "BRAVO! BRAVO!" as they threw roses at the mayor's feet.

"WE LOVE YOU, ULTRA-ROBO-MAYOR!" Superfan Teeny screamed.

"I LOVE ME, TOO!" yelled back Mayor Bossy-pants.

He tossed Awesome Dog aside and blew kisses

to the crowd. He wanted all the attention. Skyler saw it as the perfect opportunity for a sneak attack.

She had already formulated the plan as she ran to the utility shed. Skyler picked up her skateboard, hopped on, and pedaled toward a car door on the side of a junk pile. The door was tilted upright at forty-five degrees. It wasn't as smooth as a skate park ramp, but it'd still get her some air.

Skyler pushed off with her foot, then squatted low on her board. She used the car door as a ramp and flew off the edge. She soared toward the back of ultra-robo-mayor. He had no idea she was coming.

In a midair 180 spin, Skyler grabbed her skateboard off her feet and swung it at Mayor

Bossypants's head. Just as it was about to make contact—

Mayor Bossypants took a bow for his fans. Skyler whiffed. She sailed over the ultra-robo-mayor and crashed into the dirt.

"HEY! NO CHEATING!" whined the ultra-robo-mayor. "Sneak attacks are definitely against final boss fight rules! Which I just made up!"

Referee Teeny jogged out and threw a penalty flag in the air.

ILLEGAL USE OF A REALLY COOL SKATEBOARD TRICK IN A SNEAK ATTACK! AUTOMATIC REMOVAL FROM BOSS FIGHT!

The ultra-robo-mayor's shoulder T-shirt cannon fired at Skyler. She was instantly wrapped in an extra-extra-extra-small T-shirt.

The mayor looked down and said, "Second trick: stay!"

CHAPTER 26

Final Round

THE KIDS HAD a losing record of 0–2 against Mayor Bossypants. Awesome Dog's computer was fried, and Skyler was trapped in a T-shirt. Marty and Ralph would have to get creative if they were going to beat the ultra-robo-mayor.

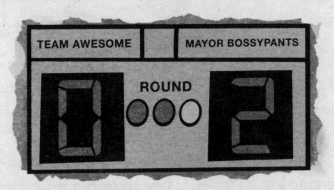

"He's too overpowered. We need to find a weapon to help us," said Marty.

The boys dug through a nearby scrap pile.

They found a beat-up car stereo, a bent license plate, and a few hubcaps.

"Check it out! A sword!" said Ralph. He drew a silver blade from the junk. He wielded it in the air like a victorious knight . . . then lowered the blade. "Mmm. Never mind. It's a windshield wiper."

"Keep searching. I'll distract him," said Marty. He picked up a hubcap and called out to the ultra-robo-mayor, "Think fast, Lead Head!"

Marty gave a full body heave. He flicked the hubcap like a Frisbee. It flew through the air, and it landed with a—

Tink! The hubcap bounced off the mayor's chest without so much as a scratch.

"I'm solid steel, dummy. It'll take more than some flimsy junk to hurt me," said the ultra-robo-mayor. He launched an extra-extra-extra-small T-shirt and trapped Marty, too.

Mayor Bossypants turned his attention back to Awesome Dog. Fives was in a glitched-out daze. The ultra-robo-mayor clenched his hand into a giant metallic fist. He slowly raised it over Awesome Dog's head. He was going to pulverize him. Mayor Bossypants said, "Final trick: play dead."

"Don't you dare hurt him!" yelled Skyler.

She and Marty kicked and pulled at their souvenir T-shirts, but the cotton held firm. The kids were helpless to stop the ultra-robo-mayor. Awesome Dog and the kids were outmatched. The ultra-robo-mayor was bigger. The ultra-robo-mayor was faster. The ultra-robo-mayor was stronger. The ultra-robo-mayor was—

Not as smart as Ralph.

"Fun fact! Steel is made from a combination of iron and carbon," said Ralph.

The mayor glanced over to see him standing by the compactor crane. Ralph flipped a switch on the control panel and said, "And iron is magnetic!"

A buzz sounded above the ultra-robo-mayor.

He looked up and scowled. Ralph had positioned the crane's magnetic plate directly over his head. Mayor Bossypants's whole body started floating off the ground. The cyborg twisted and flailed as the magnet pulled him upward. He yelled out, "NO! NO! NO! NOT FAIR!"

He ignited his firework boots to fly away, but the magnet was too strong. His suit's thick steel armor made him extra magnetic.

The ultra-robo-mayor gritted his teeth and pushed his boots to their max speed. The thrusters popped off a flurry of blue, green, and red sparkles. He was fighting so hard against the magnetism that his mechanical suit started to rattle from the stress. It cracked and split at the seams. Then it broke apart.

Piece by piece, the armor plating was peeled off his body. His quad-zooka was ripped from his arm. His shoulder cannon was torn free. Finally, his boots were yanked off his feet. He was stripped of all his high-tech gadgets. Without the metal exo-frame, Mayor Bossypants's belly flopped to the dirt. He was wearing only his Chi-Chi-Mookipon underwear.

CHAPTER 27

Overtime

WITH THE ULTRA-ROBO-MAYOR defeated, Ralph used the windshield-wiper sword to cut his friends out of their T-shirt traps.

"Smart thinking with the magnet, Ralph," said Skyler.

"Remind me to thank Carlos Cruz when we go back to school. His Attracto Glove invention gave me the idea," said Ralph.

The kids ran over to help Awesome Dog next. His head swayed as he sang, "BARK. BARK. HOW MUCH IS THAT DOGGIE IN THE WINDOW? BARK. BARK. THE ONE WITH THE SATELLITE TAIL!"

Ralph reconnected the Funstation controller to the leash for a systems check. "The damage is pretty bad, but not permanent. He'll be okay once I dry him off and reboot him. Give me a sec," explained Ralph.

"Good," said Marty. "When it's done, Fives can fly the mayor back to the police station."

"You sure about that, Marty? Someone might see Awesome Dog," asked Skyler.

Marty flashed a grin and said, "I think it's time this city knows it has some heroes protecting it."

Skyler did a happy dance. She had been waiting for Marty to say that. It was better than any apology he could have given her. She punched the air and screamed at the top of her lungs, "FROM ZEROES CLUB TO HEROES CLUB!"

Mayor Bossypants cut off her celebration. "I'm not going anywhere, and you can't make me!" The mayor was surrounded by a swarm of teenies. "I have an army of devoted and loyal assistants who will fight to the death if anyone tries to lay a finger on me!"

"Really?!" Marty asked in disbelief. "Another boss fight?! Ugh. Can't we just end this thing and go home already?"

"BARK. BARK. SYSTEMS REBOOTED!" said Awesome Dog.

Awesome Dog's eye lights were shining bright yellow, and his tail wagged. He was back to his awesome self. His now-repaired sensors spotted the teeny-tinies. His eyes switched to crosshairs.

"BARK. BARK. THREAT DETECTED. BARK. BARK. SMALL TARGETS ACQUIRED."

All the teenies stuck up their hands in surrender. Toughstuff Teeny said, "US QUIT JOB."

The mayor was stunned. He had lost his robot suit. He had lost his assistants. He didn't even have a police force to command because he'd trapped them all with extra-extra-extra-small T-shirts!

"But . . . but . . . but I was going to rule the world," pouted Mayor Bossypants. His bottom lip quivered. His eyes filled with tears. He threw himself onto his back and began kicking and screaming like a full-grown man-baby, "WAAAAAAAH! I WANTED TO BE EEEEEEPIC! WAAAAAAAH!"

Marty was relieved. *That* was the true ending of Mayor Bossypants.

CHAPTER 28

And Then This Other Stuff Happened . . .

AWESOME DOG FLEW CIRCLES around Mayor Bossypants and the teeny-tinies, lassoing them with his leash. He jetted them all back to town and air-dropped them onto the front steps of the police station. At first, there was some confusion because none of the police officers seemed to have arms. But then Awesome Dog helped to free them from their tiny T-shirt prisons, and law and order resumed.

The mayor and his assistants were arrested for the crimes of T-shirting police officers and attempted supervillainry. They were all sent to jail in matching jumpsuits. It was adorable.

With Mayor Bossypants behind bars, Townville had to hold a special election to replace him. This time the citizens voted in a truly great person,

Gal Goodlady. She had run on three campaign promises—which were very familiar, yet slightly different:

 CREATE NEW JOBS! CLEAN UP THE CITY! AND HELP THE NEEDY!

On her first day in office, Mayor Goodlady didn't recruit a team of assistants. Instead, she created new jobs by hiring construction workers to tear down the rest of Bossypants's statue. She cleaned up the city by rebuilding all the businesses that had been bulldozed. Townville rejoiced. Mayor Goodlady had truly helped all those in need.

Marty, Skyler, and Ralph were glad to be rid of Mayor Bossypants, too. Now they could get back to focusing on more important things, like buying the gold deluxe edition of *Sheriff Turbo-Karate* 2.

The Monday after the junkyard showdown, Nikola Tesla Elementary held an awards assembly in the gym. The Zeroes Club sat together on the floor as Mrs. Taylor took the microphone.

"Before we announce the science fair winners, I'd like to make a quick mention about the invention that crashed into the bathroom," said Mrs. Taylor. "As luck would have it, the school was planning on remodeling the gym this winter, so it actually saved us time and money removing that wall. Thanks to the student with the big biceps and the one with the Sherlock Holmes hat. And now I present the winner of the science fair and the one-hundred-dollar grand prize!"

Marty, Skyler, and Ralph bit their bottom lips. They squealed in excitement.

Mrs. Taylor continued. "This winning invention was one of the most original ideas the judges had ever seen."

Marty, Skyler, and Ralph shared a knowing grin.

"It's an invention that will come in very handy in the future. . . ."

The Zeroes Club bounced up and down.

"And it wowed the judges with its amazing power of transformation!" Mrs. Taylor concluded.

Marty, Skyler, and Ralph all gasped. Mrs. Taylor

had said "transformation." Now they were certain the Slop-peroni Pizza Oven was going to win!

Then Mrs. Taylor finally announced, "The winner is . . ." She paused. "The Snail Squad!"

Marty, Skyler, and Ralph leapt up with fist pumps—and immediately realized what she'd said. The Zeroes Club looked to each and said, "Snail Squad?!"

They had lost. The "transformation" Mrs. Taylor had referred to was transforming snail thoughts into words. Not slop into pizza.

The Snail Squad was presented a check for a hundred dollars. One of the squad's pets said, "OH YEAH, BOOOOOOOY! WE GOT A FAT STACK OF CASH, YO!"

"Let's give a round of applause to the winners and *all* the students who competed in the science fair," said Mrs. Taylor. "For your participation, each science team will receive a five-dollar gift card to All-Mart!!"

"Fun fact," Ralph mumbled. "Now we only need sixty-five dollars to buy the gold deluxe edition of *Sheriff Turbo-Karate 2*."

Another lightbulb sparked in Marty's head, but it wasn't for a new invention. He said, "Ya know, if we're supposed to be a new team of heroes, maybe we start with that gift card."

CHAPTER 29

Gift Card Heroes

AFTER SCHOOL, Marty, Ralph, and Skyler went to All-Mart so that they could buy the most heroic item in the store that cost less than their five-dollar gift card. It was in the gardening section. Marty selected a packet of seeds.

"Your big heroic idea is some flowers?" asked Skyler.

Marty showed her. They weren't *some* flowers. The packet was filled with marigold seeds. Skyler and Ralph instantly knew what Marty's "heroic" plan was.

They went to the house on the dead-end street. It was the same house where they had chased down spybot #1. Marty rang the doorbell. Granny Nunchucks opened the door.

"Hello, ma'am," said Marty. "We'd like to re-plant your flower garden for you."

The granny squinted at the kids through her glasses, then looked at her wrecked garden. She busted out her nun-chucks and twirled them around. She asked, "And why would you do that for me?"

"Because, uh . . ." Marty hesitated his answer.

He was nervous about telling her the truth, but he knew he had to do it. After everything the kids had gone through, Marty had learned that being a hero wasn't just about fighting cyborgs. It was about facing your problems and doing the right thing, no matter how hard it is. That's what "rising to the challenge" truly meant.

Marty took a deep breath. "Well, ma'am, me and my friends want to fix your garden because . . . well . . . you see . . ."

Skyler gave Marty a little nudge to spit it out.

"We're the ones who ruined it," he finally said.

"Fun fact! Marigolds bloom in less than eight weeks!" added Ralph. "We can have your flower bed back in shape in no time!"

Granny Nunchucks whipped her nunchucks around her body. She said through a frown, "Fun fact or not, ruining an old woman's garden is a very mean thing to do!"

Marty took a big gulp and choked back his fear. He didn't make an excuse. He was prepared to face the consequences, no matter what.

SPECIAL MOVES
➡ NUNCHUCKS POWER UPPERCUT
➡ TORNADO ROUNDHOUSE KICK
➡ SEWING A NICE QUILT

SPECIAL MOVES
➡ RUN AWAY IN FEAR
➡ HIDE IN CLOSET
➡ TRY NOT TO PEE IN PANTS

"However . . . ," said the granny. Her icy-cold frown melted into a warm smile. "Taking responsibility for your mistakes is quite commendable, young man. It's a good quality to have. To tell you the truth, I'm just happy that garden goblins haven't invaded the neighborhood."

The kids spent the afternoon fixing the granny's garden. Marty gathered the old torn-up flower stems in the front yard. Skyler resoiled the flower bed. Ralph buried the seeds and watered the rows. The kids even mowed Granny Nunchucks's front yard and backyard as a bonus.

After all their hard work, Granny Nunchucks brought out a pitcher of well-earned homemade lemonade. Marty, Skyler, and Ralph enjoyed a cool drink as they sat on the steps of her front porch.

Marty smiled and said, "Ya know, I think I can get used to this hero thing."

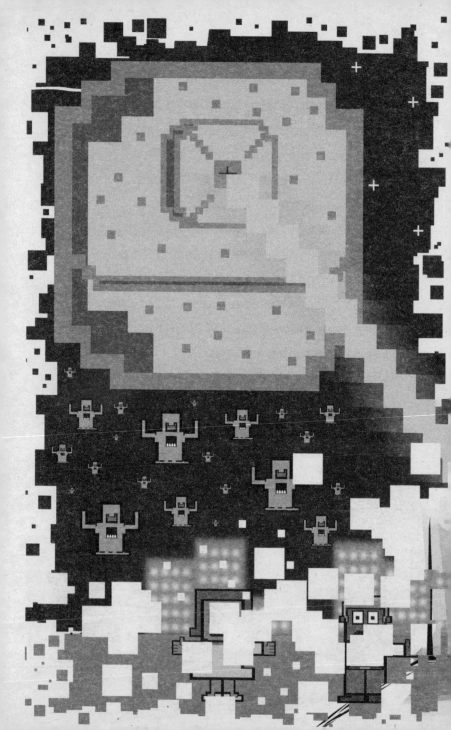

CHAPTER 30

A Second Chance

IT IS THE YEAR 3002, and the galaxy is at war for second time. . . .

The alien slime ninjas have returned, and they are really mad about losing the last war. They've—

"Check it out!" said Marty.

Ralph tapped the space bar on the keyboard to pause the internet trailer for *Sheriff Turbo-Karate 2* on HQ-0's wall of monitors. Ralph, Skyler, and Awesome Dog had been watching it on repeat. Even though they didn't have enough money for the gold deluxe edition, they were still obsessed with the game. Ralph's birthday was in a few months. There was still hope.

Marty had run in from the elevator with a magazine. "My mom got this in the mail today!" he said.

It was the new issue of *Epic Human Monthly*. Except that "Human" was crossed out, and underneath, in bold type, the magazine had printed the word "Canine." The cover showed Awesome Dog flying through the sky. His leash-lasso was carrying Mayor Bossypants and the teeny-tinies. The headline read TOWNVILLE'S NEWEST HERO! SYMBOL OF COURAGE.

"BARK. BARK. FAMOUS MODE ACTIVATED," said Awesome Dog.

"Secret's out now," said Skyler. "What's the story say?"

When Marty opened the magazine, an envelope dropped out from between the pages and fell onto the floor. The letter didn't have a return address. FOR THE ZEROES CLUB was the only thing typed across the front. Ralph picked up the envelope and tore it open. Inside, there was a shiny gold paper. It read:

Certificate of Completion

You discovered all 30 spybots.
Congratulations,
Marty, Skyler, and Ralph!

"With all this Mayor Bossypants nonsense, we totally forgot about finding out who sent the spy-bots!" said Marty.

"Wait. What's that?" asked Skyler.

She noticed something on the other side of the certificate. There was a strange gear-shaped emblem above thirty numbered blank spaces.

"It must be some kind of secret message, like a code where you match the numbers with letters," Marty guessed.

Ralph looked over the certificate. After a thorough inspection, he said, "Huh. Puzzles like this are supposed to have some sort key or symbol as a guide."

"OH! OH! OH!" Skyler tapped at the magazine in Marty's hands. "The headline! It says 'Symbol of Courage'! Symbol! Like a symbol as a guide!"

The kids searched the cover. It didn't take them long to discover the gear-shaped emblem in the background of the photograph. The emblem was identical to the one on the certificate, but it had the letter "D" in its center.

"Holy moon cheese!" said Ralph. "Someone must've put symbols all over town with different letters. If we find them all, we can decode the message."

"Okay. Thirty blank spaces, thirty mystery emblems. Time for another walk, Fives," said Marty.

Awesome Dog's leash extended from his collar. Marty picked it up and plugged into the Funstation controller. The heads-up display appeared on the screen. Awesome Dog was all systems go.

Marty handed the controller to Skyler and said, "Here. I think you should drive."

WANT TO HELP THE ZEROES CLUB DECODE THE MESSAGE?

You can go back to the start of this story and find all the mystery emblems hidden throughout Townville.

There are thirty chapters, and one mystery emblem in each of them. Every emblem has a unique letter in its center. Once you find an emblem, write its letter in the code's blank space that matches the chapter number where you found it.

These mystery emblems are blended into their surroundings, so you'll have to look carefully to find them. Emblems might be gigantic or tiny, spray-painted across a billboard or printed on the side of a lunch box.

Here's a hint to get you started in chapter 1: "Don't stop searching!"

THINK YOU CAN FIND ALL THIRTY MYSTERY EMBLEMS?

$\overline{1}\ \overline{2}\ \overline{3}\ \overline{4}\ \overline{5}\ \overline{6}$

$\overline{7}\ \overline{8}\ \overline{9}\ \overline{10}\ \overline{11}$

$\overline{12}\ \overline{13}\ \overline{14}\ \overline{15}\ \overline{16}\ \overline{17}$

$\overline{18}\ \overline{19}\ \quad \overline{20}\ \overline{21}\ \overline{22}$

$$\overline{23}\ \overline{24}\ \overline{25}\ \overline{26}\ \overline{27}\ \overline{28}\ \overline{29}\ \overset{D}{\overline{30}}$$

ABOUT THE AUTHOR

Fun fact! Justin Dean is an award-winning writer who's made stuff for television, animation, video games, and now books. When he's not coming up with funny stories, he teaches creative writing to kids. Justin lives in Los Angeles with his wife and two children. Unfortunately, they don't have any robot pets (yet).

⊙ @jddean5000

▶ Awesome Draw 5000

HOLY MOON CHEESE!

Awesome Dog and his pals face off against an army of robotic kitty toys in the AWESOMEST Awesome Dog yet!

Check out this sneak peek of . . .

The Secret Stash

"FUN FACT!" SAID RALPH. "A teenager in New Mexico once found a ten-thousand-year-old asteroid in the sand with one of these things."

"It feels like we've been out *here* for ten thousand years," groaned Skyler. "Maybe it's broken."

Marty waved a metal detector over the grass. The Zeroes Club had borrowed it from Ralph's garage. They hoped it would locate the buried secret stash.

"It works. We just haven't found the right spot yet," said Marty.

The kids had spent all afternoon scanning the back-

yard. There had been a steady hiss of static. Nothing had set off a signal.

"BARK. BARK. SWITCHING FROM SOLAR POWER TO

RESERVE BATTERY," said Awesome Dog. His eye lights clicked on as the sun went down.

"It's time we go with plan B," said Skyler. "We dig up the entire backyard. No stone unturned. No worm kicked out of its house."

"Does the 'B' in your plan B stand for 'bonkers'?" asked Marty. "Because my mom will lose it if we do that. We already blew up her front yard with a missile last month."

Ralph held up a finger. "And we all learned a valuable lesson that day: always be careful when playing fetch with Awesome Dog."

Marty pulled the "secret message" certificate from a pocket of his shorts. The header on the gold paper was a gear emblem with a question mark in its center. He reread the message aloud: "'Secret stash buried in the backyard.' Hmm. There's got to be more to this puzzle."

Marty squinted. All this mystery stuff was giving him a stress headache. He rubbed his temples with his thumbs.

"Hey, what if we do plan C," offered Ralph. "We call off the search for the night, and we 'C' if we can figure this out tomorrow with fresh eyes."

Skyler jumped in on the plan. "Yeah. You guys can come over to my house for dinner. My dad can make us his special kimchi pizza again."

Marty didn't respond. He didn't even turn around. It wasn't because he didn't like Mr. Kwon's cooking. He was focused on something else. His head was cocked to the side as he stared at a nearby tree.

"What's he doing?" Skyler asked Ralph.

"Seeing something with fresh eyes," said Marty. "There wasn't anything else to the puzzle. We were just trying to solve it at the wrong time of day."

He pointed to the tree trunk. There was a green gear with a question mark in the center. It was written in glow-in-the-dark paint!

Gear Marks the Spot

THE KIDS HAD FOUND WHERE the secret stash was buried, but shovels wouldn't be needed. They had their very own heavy-duty excavator.

Marty pointed to the base of the tree with the gear emblem. "Fives, dig here!"

"BARK. BARK. ARCHAEOLOGY MODE ACTIVATED," said Awesome Dog.

The robot dog's wrists began rotating like two drills. There was a whirling *zzzzzzzzz* sound as they spun faster. Fives pressed his paws to the grass and burrowed under the tree. He

emerged, covered in dirt, a few feet away. In his mouth he was carrying a case by its handle.

Ralph took the case from Awesome Dog and tapped on the hard plastic exterior. "Explains why the metal detector didn't get a signal," he said.

The side of the case was marked: BEWARE! CONTENTS ARE

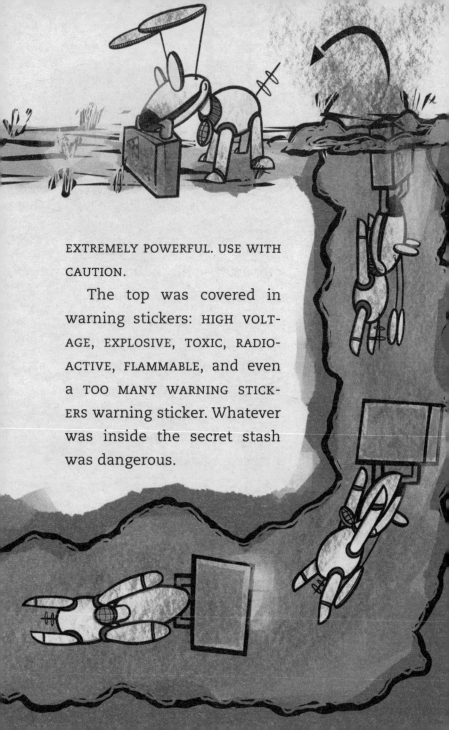

EXTREMELY POWERFUL. USE WITH CAUTION.

The top was covered in warning stickers: HIGH VOLTAGE, EXPLOSIVE, TOXIC, RADIOACTIVE, FLAMMABLE, and even a TOO MANY WARNING STICKERS warning sticker. Whatever was inside the secret stash was dangerous.

Marty took a step back.

Ralph nervously bit his bottom lip.

Skyler's jaw dropped.

Then she let out a giddy laugh. She yelled,

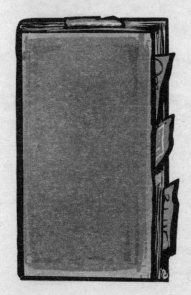

"JACKPOT!" as she grabbed the case from Ralph and pried it open. But her smile quickly faded. Inside was a thick leather-bound book.

And that was it.

"That better be a book of magic spells that summons zombies with eye lasers or something, or I am going to be *very* disappointed," said Skyler.

Marty opened the book. The top half of the first page had been torn out. There was the tail end of a handwritten entry: "—just follow the directions."

just follow the directions

"It's some kind of diary," said Marty.

"Better be a wizard's diary," muttered Skyler.

They thumbed through the pages. There were scribbled notes, advanced equations, chemical mixtures, machine schematics, a map of the city, computer coding, some—

"Wait a second," said Ralph. "I've seen that before." He flipped back to a diagram of a cylinder attached to a bent pole. "Do you two realize what this is?"

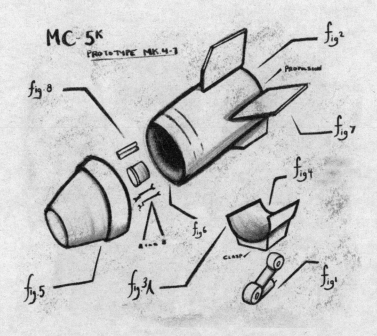

Marty guessed, "A fancy thermos holder?"

"Activate mega-cannon!" ordered Ralph.

"BARK. BARK. ACTIVATING ATOMIC MEGA-CANNON," said Fives. The hatch on his back opened. The metal arm that folded out held a cylindrical missile.

"This book isn't just a diary. This is the diary of the guy who created Fives," said Ralph. "We've got the blueprints for all his inventions."

Marty looked to Skyler and asked, "Still disappointed?"

FiND YOUR VOiCE
WiTH ONE OF THESE EXCiTiNG GRAPHIC NOVELS

PRESENTED BY RH 📖 GRAPHIC

1447

YEARLING

Turning children into readers for more than fifty years.

Classic and award-winning literature for every shelf.
How many have you checked out?